GRACE'S GHOSTS

Stephenie Wilson Peterson

Appropriate for Teens, Intriguing to Adults

Immortal Works LLC
1505 Glenrose Drive
Salt Lake City, Utah 84104
Tel: (385) 202-0116

Cover Art by Ashley Literski
http://strangedevotion.wixsite.com/strangedesigns

ISBN 978-1-7343866-2-2 (Paperback)
ASIN B083RR3LFM (Kindle Edition)

For Nick,

For always supporting me, for believing in me more than I believe in myself, for never letting me quit. Thank you. I love you forever.

GHOST GIRL

I'd never been afraid of ghosts. Actually, it was quite the opposite. I was more comfortable with the dead than with the living. The many ghosts of the tiny mountain town of Tansy had followed me as long as I could remember. Ghosts, unlike people, never bothered me a bit.

It was the living, with their cliques and their judgment, who made my skin crawl. Sixth grade hadn't been easy for me. Not that any year of my education had been pleasant. Let's just say that kids who see the dead weren't exactly considered cool at my school. My outsider status with the living was well-established: I was the strange kid who talked to people who weren't there. But the living citizens of my town were the ones who were missing an entire world. I was the only one who knew Tansy's biggest secret. You're never truly alone in this town. Though few people live here, thousands spent their afterlives here.

I managed to avoid uttering a single word to another living person for the first half of my last day of sixth grade. Slouching in my chair in the back row, I hoped to go unnoticed by the other kids. Less than three hours of school remained before summer freed me from their torment for eight whole weeks.

Most of the time, I didn't mind my outsider status. I had friends. They just lacked heartbeats. It was hard to be the weird girl in school, but I always had my cat, Midnight, by my side, rubbing up against my ankles when some bratty kid tormented me.

Midnight was dead. He didn't run in front of a car, die of old age, or get attacked by a coyote in the woods. He had always been dead, at least as long as I'd known him. Midnight was a ghost.

Since only 204 people lived in Tansy, the school was tiny. The same seven kids had been in my grade since kindergarten, and even though they lumped all of the fourth through sixth graders in one classroom, there were still only twenty students in the room. You'd think I'd have a shot at ducking under the radar and just chilling with Midnight, who was, as always, curled up in an invisible ball by my feet. But that wasn't possible in Tansy.

Tara Gleason and her pack of annoying "cool girls" knew they wouldn't get a chance to torture me for a while. Just after lunch, Tara made sure to make me suffer one last time before the term ended. Tossing her blonde braid over her shoulder, she sauntered up to me, snatched my yearbook off my desk, and flipped through it. My shoulders tensed, but I didn't dare speak. I just stared at my tormentor with my jaw set.

"Well, let's see! Who's signed Grace's yearbook?" Tara said in a mockingly sweet voice. "Hmm. Has Holly signed it?" She paused, pretending to search for a signature she knew the book didn't contain. "Nope. Holly didn't sign it. What about Amy? Hmm. She didn't either. Lily didn't. Sophie didn't." Tara turned a few more pages. "And you know *I* didn't sign it yet, either," she added, her voice turning cruel. "Almost no one has signed your yearbook, Gross Grace. I think the only one who signed it was Bain." She cackled and shot a look at the only kid in class who ever said a kind word to me.

Bain Bello was a bit of an outsider. He fit in with the other kids a little better than I did, but he tended to speak in riddles and rhymes, always wore black, and kept his hair long, which made him stand out from the other kids. While the other kids teased Bain, it never seemed to faze him. The result was that they ignored him more often than not. I wouldn't call him my friend, but he was always civil to me. He smiled weakly and shook his head to let me know he thought Tara was a jerk.

"That's fine," I told Tara, reaching for the book. Midnight hissed at her, but his protest found its way to my ears alone.

"No, no, no. That won't do at all! We *must* sign your yearbook!" Tara turned, strutting back to the front of the classroom like she was on the catwalk and her blue and yellow cheer uniform was all that. My stomach sank. I tried to convince myself it wouldn't be that bad. Maybe she'd just write something generic like, "Have a good summer." But my gut said otherwise.

Giggling wafted through the classroom as Tara and her posse passed my yearbook back and forth all afternoon long. The hair on my arms stood on end with each high-pitched squeal. Those girls were up to no good, and I was powerless to stop them.

And this time, I was truly on my own. Sometimes, when a kid barked rude comments at me, the ghost of Thomas Meyer snagged their scissors or knocked their notebooks off their desks. Once, when Tara tripped me in the hallway, the spirit of Polly Hansen pulled her seat out from under her no less than six times in an hour. Many of the spirits looked out for me during the school day. Of course, the bully never knew they'd lost their pencil because of a paranormal prank, but I always smiled slyly while I watched their hopeless search.

Other than Midnight, however, the ghosts were absent from school most of the day, leaving me alone with my thoughts. Sometimes, they did this when I had an important test to take or some other reason I needed to concentrate. It's hard making it through the school day with ghosts all around. It made me stand out even more than I already did.

Even if they did make me seem like a freak, the ghosts were my best friends. For as long as I could remember, spirits surrounded me. The ghosts say I babbled at them non-stop as an infant. As a toddler, I played hide-and-seek with my ghostly friends. While most kids cried on the first day of kindergarten as they parted ways with their mothers, I didn't mind at all. Five spirits accompanied me on my first day of school.

My stomach flipped, when, about twenty minutes from the final bell, Tara dropped the book back on my desk, leaned in so close to me I could smell her cherry Chapstick, and whispered, "Fixed it."

I stared at the yearbook like it contained the Ebola virus. I avoided reading it for several minutes, trying to distract myself with Midnight, wondering if I could spend some time with the ghosts after school. I ran my finger over the smooth, glossy spine of the book. *It can't be that bad,* I thought, forcing myself to open it up.

It was even worse than I'd expected. Page after page was covered in insults.

Gross Grace is a loser.

Why do you always talk to yourself? Oh right, because we all hate you!

Dear Grace, I'm so sorry that you are so ugly. With all of your gray clothes and glasses, you look like an undertaker. Maybe your parents can give you a makeover for your birthday. You need it.

Every single time my name appeared in the book, they crossed it off and wrote "Gross Grace." They'd added devil horns to my photo, the dark ink appearing to come out of my wild black curls. I sat looking at my own thin, pale face, my weak smile seeming to say, "What did you expect?" I noticed for the first time the reflection of a ghost on the lenses of my glasses. Everyone else probably thought it was the flash, but I knew better.

Flipping through the pages, I read the insults, again and again, hoping that somewhere within the book's pages I'd find something to make me feel better. But the notes only held unkind words, save for the short note Bain had left before Tara got her hands on it.

Thomas Meyer appeared next to my desk just as I snapped the book shut. Where had he been earlier when he could have interfered? Or he could have at least comforted me while I waited to get my book back.

"Hello, Grace!" he said, smiling, oblivious to my pain. "Some of the ghosts and I have something to discuss with you. I don't want to interrupt your last day of school, so can we drop by tomorrow morning?"

"Yeah," I told him as tears welled hot in my eyes. The bell rang just then, releasing me from my prison for the next eight weeks. I headed home alone, glad to put an end to another horrible year at Tansy School.

On any given morning, I expected to find a spirit or two waiting for me to wake up. The dead are chattier than you'd think, especially since I was the only one in town who could see and talk to them. But when I roused just after daybreak on my first day of summer vacation, spirits lined my room from wall-to-wall. I opened my mouth, but no sound came out.

The sheer volume of ghosts rendered me speechless. There must have been one hundred of them crammed on top of my bookcase, floating above my window seat, and pretty much filling every inch of air space my small, gray-walled room had to offer. I gasped, sat up in bed, and grabbed my glasses off my nightstand.

A dozen or so ghastly faces floated just above my eyes, which, let me tell you, is a startling sight before the sun has fully risen. Everywhere I turned, more haunts wafted nearby, eagerly waiting in the early morning light.

This wasn't how I expected my day to start. Puzzled, I wondered if I might still be sleeping. *That's it. This is a weird dream,* I thought as I yanked my heavy gray quilt over my face. Underneath the covers, I squeezed my eyes shut as tight as possible and prayed that I'd only imagined the hoard of haunts in my bedroom. I didn't exactly expect my summer vacation to start this way, especially not at dawn.

Inching out of the quilt, I opened my eyes just a slit and exhaled. Ghosts still filled every nook and cranny of my room. I shook my head, then shook out my sheets as if it might scare the spooks away. This, of course, didn't work. I knew it wouldn't, but I'm not exactly what you would call a morning person. These spirits were my friends, even if this overzealous early morning visit annoyed me a bit. I sat back up in bed. The ghosts rarely possessed this level of enthusiasm. The least I could do was listen.

Before I could decide what to say to the ghosts, Thomas Meyer floated to the foot of my bed. Thomas, a round-faced ghost who had been haunting Tansy longer than any of the others, died at only fourteen years old. He gave off a youthful vibe, though technically, he was over three hundred years old.

"Good morning, Grace. I told you a few of us would be by to visit, but judging by the expression on your face, you forgot."

That's right. I'd pretty much forgotten all about our conversation as soon as I got out of the school building the day before.

Thomas, however, clearly didn't forget. He looked down at me impatiently as I thought about the previous day.

"Right, sorry. I just...didn't expect so many of you."

Midnight appeared on my bed and stared at me with bright eyes.

"Grace," Thomas began, "You know that you're the only one who can see us, and no one else has as long as I've been dead."

I nodded.

Thomas continued. "I do not have to tell you that the spirits who reside in this town are ready to move on, and I think I've discovered what it is that imprisons so many souls in Tansy."

My heart skipped a beat. I'd always known something wasn't right about my town. The spirits spent many an hour lamenting to me about being trapped in Tansy, but no one could ever give me an answer when I tried to figure out why Tansy was so different from other places. I sat straighter and tried to listen to what my friend had to say.

"We are not supposed to stay in this spot for eternity. We're supposed to go on to the Light. To Heaven. To be with our loved ones who came before us. We've long suspected that we were cursed. But we could not prove it. Until now."

Cursed? As in witchcraft? Is that even real? Too shocked to speak, I nodded at Thomas to continue.

"A few weeks ago, Polly started haunting the bank. They have a large old attic space that's been unoccupied for a few hundred years. It's a nice gathering place for the younger spirits."

One of my closest friends, Polly Hansen, who passed as a pre-teen, wafted across the room so that she hovered next to Thomas and nodded.

"I found an old letter up there. It was to the bankers from a woman named Lavina. In it, she promised to curse the town," Polly said.

"And you think she could have? Can people really curse one another?"

"We're cursed, Grace. Why else do you think so many ghosts would be in a single town? Some of us never even lived in Tansy. Several of the spirits only passed through the town a time or two when alive, and yet they found themselves forever here in the afterlife," Thomas said, nodding to the permanently six-year-old spirit of Jenni Duncan.

Jenni died in a car crash when she was a kindergartener in the late 1980s. She'd only been to Tansy once before her death, but she'd spent more than thirty years in the town since her death. Her family had survived the crash, so she spent her afterlife missing them.

"Um...okay," I said, trying to comprehend his words. "So you're telling me that magic exists, and I am supposed to figure out how to undo a spell?" I couldn't help but shake my head at the absurdity of it all.

"Of course magic exists," he told me as simply as if he'd told me the sky was blue or that April comes before May.

My head swam as I tried to come to terms with what he was saying. "You're cursed. Trapped in Tansy. I guess that explains why

I've never seen so many spirits in another city. And why so many of you don't have strong ties to the town. But what do you expect *me* to do?" A lump formed in my throat, and I swallowed hard, trying to push it, and my fears, back down.

Thomas' translucent face twisted into a frown, and I knew I'd hurt his feelings. I took a breath and tried to explain myself. "I'm just a kid, and I know nothing about magic. I don't think I *can* break a curse."

"You're alive, Grace," Thomas replied. "That gives you all the advantage."

I tried to consider what Thomas told me as the galley of ghosts chimed in with their thoughts and encouragement, which, to be honest, made it hard to think.

"We need help, and you are the only one who can save us," begged Mrs. Mooney, an old woman who taught me piano back when I was six, and she was, well, *alive*.

"Please, Grace. I miss my Grammy," Jenni said, her high ponytail bobbing as she bounced.

"We've been waiting a long time, Grace. We need your help," pleaded Polly.

"We beg you," boomed Bartholomew Foster, his voice low and rattly. He was another one of my friends, a beefy kid with dark voids where his eyes should have been. Though I often wondered, I never dared to ask him what happened to his eyes.

All of the eyes in the room started intently at me, full of expectation. I didn't know what they thought I could do, but they seemed desperate for my help. If they needed me, I knew I would at least have to try. I looked down, squishing my soft gray pillow, trying to think of what I could do.

"I want to help all of you, but I am having a hard time understanding all of this. Curses, magic. It's not exactly something they taught me at Tansy School."

"Another failure of the education system," Thomas sighed. "Curses and magic are all over the Fantasma Mountains. Magic is woven into the very land upon which this town was built. But the dead are unable to do anything about it," Thomas said.

"And I can?" My pulse quickened.

"You can see us and talk to us. You're also able to lift objects off the ground, talk to the living, and leave the town," Polly said, her long ringlets bouncing as she spoke.

Midnight let out a long meow and rubbed his back against my leg, sending a chill through me.

I took in a breath and looked around the room, at all of the hopeful faces, packed in there like sardines, begging me to help them. They did not make it easy to say no. My stomach rumbled.

As if my life isn't weird enough, now I have to figure out how to break a curse that may or may not exist.

"Why would this Lavina woman curse the town?" I asked.

Thomas answered for the crowd. "Some of us may have mentioned her to you before. Lavina lived just outside of town when I was alive. She was strange, and no one in town trusted her."

A flash of recognition hit me as I remembered some of the stories I'd been told about the woman. I nodded.

Thomas continued, "Everyone thought she was a witch. She tried to spend time with the townspeople, but we wanted nothing to do with her. Eventually, a group of concerned citizens banded together to ban her from our town."

A witch? I thought. *I guess they aren't just in cartoons and old books.* Thomas floated right up to me, face-to-face as I listened intently.

"I always thought they were too hard on the old woman. But I saw her the day the town banished her. She was filled with rage. Her eyes were mad with fury, and she screamed that we had made a mistake. Shortly after she left, I died. I was unable to move on to the Light. And eventually, many other souls piled up in Tansy. I always thought it was suspicious, but I had no proof."

"But then I found the letter, and it all fell into place," Polly chimed in.

I understood why the ghosts would think the scorned witch would be angry enough to curse the town of Tansy. Still, I didn't know what to do with this information. As I looked out into the crowd of gray faces, a sense of hopelessness washed over me. Heat rose up into my cheeks. How was I going to help them? Their desperation to move on to the Light was obvious, but I didn't have a clue as to what I should do next.

Finally, I stood, accidentally passing through Mrs. Mooney, who let out a startled gasp. Ghosts don't like it when people walk through them. I wasn't a big fan of it either. It felt all cold and tingly. I gave her an apologetic shrug before I spoke.

"I'll try to help you guys. But can I at least eat breakfast first?"

The ghosts cheered so loudly that whispers were surely heard throughout Tansy. Of course, no one even thought twice about the sound. Tansy teemed with ghostly whispers that only I could understand. To me, however, the noise was deafening. I shushed the spooks, and Thomas asked me to meet them later that day in the field on the other end of town. I agreed, and I made my way downstairs without any ghostly companions, relieved to have a chance to eat my breakfast in peace.

2

SUMMER HOMEWORK FROM MY MOM AND GHOSTS

"What have I gotten myself into this time?" I muttered under my breath as I slid into my seat at the kitchen table.

"What was that, dear?" Mom asked, her head pressed up against the birdcage which housed the colorful parrot she'd owned since my infancy. Before I could answer, she turned back to Petey and gave him a cracker.

"Nothing," I replied even though I'd already lost her attention.

"Nothing. Nothing," the annoying bird repeated.

"Okay. Well, happy first day of summer!" Finally finished with her bird, Mom walked across the room and stood near me.

Dad entered the room with a newspaper in one hand and a cup of coffee in the other.

"Hey, kiddo. Mom and I bought you a few new canvases and some paints. Thought you might want to keep painting this summer since you loved that art class so much."

"Thanks, Dad."

"We were impressed with your grades and wanted to reward you," Mom said, picking up my report card from the counter and holding it up for me to see. "A 4.0 GPA should be celebrated," her brow furrowed over her gray eyes. "And maintained."

There she went, putting the academic pressure on again even though I was on break. I pulled a box of cereal out of the pantry and set it on the table. Polly floated through the kitchen, giggling and waving. I gave her a slight nod. Mom took it as a sign that I agreed with her and went on about grades for a while. I didn't dare mention that the nod was intended for my dead friend.

"...should really keep your studies up this summer. I borrowed a Spanish text from the school so that you can get ahead of your peers."

Just what I wanted. Summer homework.

"Well, I better eat breakfast first," I told her. I poured my cereal and set it on the old white farmhouse table that had been in the kitchen for generations. I leaned over my bowl, cramming cereal in my mouth as if my life depended on it. A cool sensation tickled my back as Mrs. Mooney attempted to correct my posture. Once a piano teacher, always a piano teacher, even in death.

I shot her a look to get her to stop poking me, but Mom thought the scowl was for her.

"Grace. You don't have to be rude about it. A little bit of summer Spanish won't kill you."

I didn't correct her. I generally did not mention ghosts to my parents. They didn't understand. I had tried, of course, but this always resulted in nervous glances and talk of therapy as they insisted that ghosts were not real. They didn't want to see the evidence in front of them.

Even for your average person, life in Tansy pointed to the existence of ghosts. There was always the feeling of eyes watching, but when you turned around, no one could be seen. A cool breeze would whiz by on an otherwise windless day. Whispers whirled around empty rooms. Radios and televisions never worked quite right in Tansy.

Though a myriad of reasons existed to suspect that our town was haunted, only I could confirm what the others suspected and would never, ever talk about after the age of four or five. By then, the grown-ups made sure the kids didn't talk about what made Tansy special. People in this town didn't like anything strange. Anything that stepped outside of the box. Anyone weird. *Like me.*

It was difficult for me to keep such a big part of myself from my parents, but they'd left me no choice. I tried to feel close to my parents, but, forced to act as if ghosts didn't exist around them, we grew distant. I had to keep the biggest part of myself a secret. The older I got, this secret put a larger and larger void between us, and left me feeling quite lonely in my own home, despite the fact that there were always a dozen or so ghosts haunting me.

I finished my breakfast in record time. Once I emptied my bowl, I flew up to my bedroom with my new art supplies. Sighing as I put them away, I wished for a moment to paint or draw. But the ghosts had waited centuries for my help. I didn't want to make them wait any longer.

I got dressed. Like most days, my entire outfit was gray. When I wore gray, I felt like I could walk around unnoticed, slipping into the background, away from the world of the living and blending in with the translucent gray world of the dead. I pulled my sweater over my head. Even in warm summer weather, I knew that spending time with the dead made me chilly. I paused to hear the front door close, signaling my parents' departure for the day. After a few minutes of waiting to be sure they were truly gone, I flew down the stairs.

A foreboding feeling overcame me as I opened the front door.

A FIELD OF GHOULS

I stood on my front porch for a moment as I took a deep breath, trying to calm the anxiety building in the pit of my stomach. I'd lived my whole life in the old purple house on Willow Way. The house stood in the village for generations—my grandma had grown up in the house and before that, her mother and grandmother had. For over three hundred years, it had been passed down through generations. The knowledge that the home housed so many of my family members comforted me.

Doubt roiled in the pit of my stomach. I often went above and beyond for my dead friends, probably because I didn't have any living ones. This, however, wasn't like mailing an anonymous letter to a ghost's widow to tell her that her husband missed her on their anniversary or that the key to the safe deposit box was hidden in a toolbox in the garage. This was bigger, more important, more complicated. And could I even do this? I mean, *magic?* I didn't think it existed. Then again, strange things surrounded me. If I could see ghosts, maybe I shouldn't be so quick to reject the idea of magic.

Curse or no curse, I wanted to help the spirits. They were basically family to me. When I was little, I never questioned why the many ghostly beings filled the streets of Tansy. They were just there. They always had been there. But as I grew, I realized that the ghosts stayed inside the town's walls. While they wandered freely within the village, following me to school or the small lakeside park, not a single spook nor haunt ever passed the crumbling brick wall that stood at the north end of town, even when I begged them to come with me.

When I visited other towns, I rarely saw ghosts. Of course, when I passed a cemetery, I might notice a spirit or seven swirling above the spot where they'd been laid to rest, but the next time I passed, they'd be gone. Most places possessed the occasional ghost with unfinished business who lingered, haunting a house or spooking the schoolyard, but what I saw every day in Tansy was entirely different. The more I thought about it, the more a curse made sense.

The ghosts of Tansy had always been there for me. I needed to be there for them, too.

As I stepped off the porch, a cold sensation surged up my leg.

"Hey Midnight," I said to the little black cat. "I guess you want my help, too."

Midnight mewed. The ghost cat stayed by my side every day of my life. He followed me everywhere. The benefit of having a ghost for a pet is that no one could tell me where he could or could not go. No one ever told me to get the cat out of the cafeteria or to remove my feline from class, because no one could see him. I did get odd looks as I stroked the air or scratched at empty space, but I had long since given up on being normal. Who wants to be normal, anyway? Who needs living friends when you have so many undead ones? At least, I felt that way most of the time.

Midnight and I strolled down Willow Way and turned onto Main Street. Tansy, like most of the villages in the Fantasma Mountains, was tiny and, quite frankly, boring, if not for all of the ghosts. But it was beautiful. I breathed in the fresh mountain air and paused to look at the tall peaks behind Lake Nixie. As I did, a chill shot through me as a handful of spirits flew past. The ghosts were even more active than usual as they all rushed to get to the field where Thomas had asked me to meet him. Of course, not another living person saw any of it.

Midnight and I arrived at the field. The scene before me was intimidating, even for someone who prefers the company of ghosts to that of the living.

Every single ghost of Tansy was present. The three-acre field overflowed with spirits. Thousands of them floated there, waiting for me, no more than a few inches apart. Countless gray faces gazed upon me with an intensity I couldn't shake. I had to walk through them—which both ghosts and I despised. The lack of an opening to walk through left me without any other option.

I mumbled apologies to each ghost as I stepped through them. They didn't seem to mind. I pushed through the field of ghouls, trying to find a good place to address them.

A sizable boulder stood on the south end of the field. I climbed up the cold, craggy stone and contemplated what to say to the crowd of spirits. Midnight wafted around my ankles, peering up at me, the yellow of his eyes a sharp contrast to the gray of the human ghosts. Animal spirits always presented themselves to me with glowing eyes, a trait that had always made it especially difficult for me to say no to my cat.

"Grace. Thank you so much for coming," Thomas said, wafting up to where I stood. "We're so happy to have you helping us!"

"I want to help you. Truly, I do. But I don't know how," I told him softly while the eyes of thousands of ghosts burned into me.

"I might have a place for you to start. Just past the wall on the edge of the field is a cottage. It's only half a mile or so into the forest. That's where Lavina lived. We can't go there. But you can. Maybe something remains in her cottage. Maybe a clue was left behind that could help break the witch's curse," Thomas told me.

I looked over the wall into the forest, unable to see the cabin. I realized it must be a good distance into the woods, hidden by the dense forest. The spirits swirled around me, whispering words of encouragement.

"Please look, Grace," Mrs. Mooney pleaded.

"Help us," Bartholomew begged.

"Gracie's gonna help us!" Jenni squealed, her translucent face filled with a joyful smile.

Midnight meowed his approval.

The idea of wandering through a forest until I found an abandoned home did not appeal to me, but the sea of gray faces begging me to help them was too much for me to ignore.

"I'll look. I can't promise that I'll be able to do anything, but I can promise that I will try my hardest for you all."

The field whirled with excitement. The ghosts' joy pulsed through the air as they spoke words of encouragement. *All* of them. There were so many cheers and exclamations that I couldn't hear a thing. I covered my ears but to no avail. The loud vibrations attacked my eardrums.

Polly put her fingers in her mouth, and a piercing whistle rang through the air.

"Hey! You're hurting her ears! Why don't you all head home to your haunts and let Thomas and me take it from here?"

More voices erupted from the crowd. This time they were angry at being admonished by Polly. She didn't seem to notice. She floated above all of the other ghosts, whistled once more, then shouted, "I said scoot!"

After another minute of grumbling, the ghosts dissipated, and only Polly and Thomas remained.

"Thanks, Pol."

Her gray face became a full shade brighter as she smiled. "Sometimes you just have to put them in their place."

Thomas chuckled. "They're just excited. Some of us have been waiting for three-hundred years for a hint as to why we're here."

As he spoke, his voice got quieter and quieter. Polly's head snapped toward him, concern washing over her gray face.

"Again?" she asked, her voice faltering a bit.

Thomas nodded meekly. While the ghosts were always translucent, he was becoming almost transparent. He was so light that I could barely see him. And then, he was gone.

"What's going on?" I asked, trying not to freak out.

"He's been..." Polly paused, searching for the right word, "fading."

"Fading? Does he come back?" My eyes darted around, searching for my friend.

"So far he has," Polly said.

"So far?"

"He and a few of the others who have been here longest have been having these episodes for a year or so now. As time passes, they get more and more frequent. We're all afraid that they will eventually fade away and never come back."

"Where do they go? To the Light? To Heaven?"

"Nowhere. When they fade, they're just gone. When they come back, they have no memory of the time that passed. I'm afraid that if you don't break the curse, they will cease to exist on this plane or the next."

Cease to exist. I couldn't let my friends disappear into oblivion. Time was ticking, and I knew I must save the ghosts before it was too late. The thought made my stomach lurch, and tears began to form in the corners of my eyes.

"Show me where the cabin is. I don't want to wait another minute," I said, my voice cracking.

Polly pointed out the direction of the cabin and tried to provide instructions on finding it. Of course, her landmarks were three hundred years old. As far as I could tell, everything was overgrown. Doubt crept into my mind. The cabin might not even exist anymore.

I climbed down the boulder and walked to the wall. Polly stayed put as I hopped over the low stone barrier. I peeked back over my shoulder at her as she stared after me with tears in her smoky eyes and her mouth open wide. Midnight hopped over the wall, following me into the woods.

"I thought you guys couldn't leave town." He'd never left Tansy before today. At least not when I was around.

Midnight meowed. I shrugged, thinking maybe curses worked

differently on cats. I walked into the woods, Midnight following. My mind moaned with musings. *How can I help them? Can a kid even break an old curse? And how would I even figure out if the witch really did curse them?*

Eager to help my friends, my feet pushed me forward on the mossy ground at a rapid pace, but I seemed to be going nowhere. The trees all looked the same to me. There had once been a cobblestone pathway that served as a road between Tansy and Luna. There were a few spots where the stones were visible, but shrubs and overgrown grass made them difficult to find. Polly told me that Lavina's house was not far off the path, but this information was not proving to be useful.

The air was heavy with the scent of earth and pine as I passed tree after tree, rock after rock, straining to see the remnants of the cobblestone. I walked for at least an hour. Fear churned in my belly as the realization that I had gone too far hit me.

I stopped walking. Turning in circles, I scanned the woods for any sign of a path. Nothing. I was lost in the forest. Sweat beaded up on my forehead as my heart rate accelerated. Midnight mewed and brushed against me, reminding me I wasn't totally alone in this.

The ghost cat turned and began walking back the way we came. *Seems logical enough,* I thought as I followed him. We walked back toward town (or at least I was pretty sure we were walking back toward town) for about forty-five minutes. I continued scanning the thick forest for signs of a cabin, but mostly, I was just desperate to get back to Tansy.

Midnight stopped suddenly. He looked up at me, meowed, and turned to the right. I thought the town was the other direction, but I'm no Girl Scout, so I followed the dead cat.

"Where are you going, Kitty-Cat?" I asked as he disappeared behind a towering oak. I jogged a bit to catch up with him. After I passed the enormous tree, I saw him. And the cabin.

Veiled by vines and moss, the cabin stood hidden in a cluster of trees. Years of overgrowth covered the door and windows. The roof sagged. I imagined it three hundred years ago, an adorable, cozy cabin. But now, the only word that described it was creepy.

A chill shot down my spine. I didn't want to go inside. Before that day, old places didn't scare me. This, however, felt different. I looked at my ghoulish cat by my side and said, "Here goes nothing."

With much apprehension, I approached the cabin and tore down some vines obstructing the door. I put my hand on the ancient doorknob and pulled. The decayed door let out a moan of objection, but I pushed harder, and it creaked its reluctance until it opened. I stepped through the doorway and gasped.

CABIN FEVER

I stood inside a room no living person had inhabited in over three hundred years. I squinted as my eyes adjusted to lack of daylight. The home's age and disuse were obvious. Every surface of the cramped cabin had a thick layer of dust and decay. Only small beams of light fought their way through the mess of vines and overgrowth that covered the windows. The meager rays illuminated puffs of powdery dust and served only to remind me of the level of disrepair. A mound of mushrooms grew in the middle of the muddy floor. Near the center of the home, a ray of light shone in the musty air, peeking in through a hole in the roof, illuminating the mushrooms. A tiny table teetered in the back of the room, threatening to topple any time. A rat rustled in the ruins of an old bed covered in spindly spider silk.

Yuck.

As I inched forward into the dark and dreary cabin, I feared the flimsy floorboards would fail. From each careful step sprung a scream of protest from the decrepit wood. I worried I would injure myself, and contemplated turning back, but Midnight meowed, seeming to urge me to keep going. I gazed at my feline friend, wondering what he knew.

Was Midnight around when the curse was cast? I'd often tried to guess when Midnight might have lived, but, despite the fact that he knew everything about me, I only knew what I could muse from his meows.

The cabin looked as if someone had been living her life with no intention of ever leaving it and then walked away, without ever looking back. Even all these many, many years later, a cup and plate sat on the table, as if waiting for their owner to come home for supper. Covered in dust and cobwebs, the dishes stood, defying time. On one end of the room stood a crumbling fireplace, filled with a big black cauldron green with the fuzz of many moons of moss.

A snake slithered beside my foot, and a scream slipped from my lips. Startled, the snake slipped into some unknown corner of the cabin.

Keep going, I ordered myself. Snakes terrified me for as long as I could remember, and it took every bit of my willpower to move forward into the cabin.

This dwelling was more wild than domestic; its inhabitants must have been animals and insects for hundreds of years. The smell of mildew and soil filled my nose. Try as I might to repress my reservations about the home, I was downright terrified. Something about this place didn't feel right. It was more than the fact that it was ancient and abandoned. It felt malicious—if a cabin in the woods could give off such an air.

My heart beat as if it was a bat flapping its wings to escape the hold of a captor. I pulled the sleeves of my gray sweater over my hands, took a deep breath, and moved forward. *I can do this,* I thought. *At least, I hope I can.*

Next to the bed sat a side table, and on it sat several books, dusty, mildewy, leather-bound volumes. *Books are always a good place to start,* I thought, and I crept across the room. I picked one up, blew off decades of dust, and opened it.

A Collection of Potions and Brews, the swirling text on the title page declared, betraying the secret Lavina tried so hard to hide all those years ago. There was no denying that this was a witch's cabin.

I picked up the next book. It too, told a tale of a witch in the woods. *Curses and Hexes for the Woodland Witch.*

The third book was the largest. I barely breathed as I opened it. *White Magic: How to Help and Heal.* My stomach dropped. This wasn't right.

"White Magic? Isn't that good magic? I thought she cursed the townspeople," I said aloud, though only Midnight was there to hear me. He mewed insistently as I thought about an old movie I once watched about magic. In the movie, white magic was good and black magic was bad. I let out a confused sigh as I set the three books on the bed and turned to the cat, who had made himself at home in the creepy cabin and rested peacefully on the broken-down bed.

How like a cat to make himself the king of the castle already. I laughed.

"Do you know something about this, Kitty-Cat?" I asked aloud.

Midnight meowed again. Loudly. I wondered again what he knew and wished he could tell me.

The cat whooshed across the room and stopped next to another small end table. He looked up at the tabletop and meowed again. I spied something silvery sitting on the surface of the side table. I maneuvered across the rickety floor over to my ghoul of a pet to investigate further. Midnight purred loudly as I approached.

The silvery something turned out to be a mirror. I gently gripped the handle and picked it up. Its antiqued glass was foggy and black tarnish crept around the corners. Still, it was a thing of beauty. The handle caught my eye with its with intricate swirling patterns and silver sunflowers.

Midnight meowed again as I held the mirror. With the cold metal of the handle in my hand, power vibrated through me. For the first time all day, I felt something other than overwhelmed and terrified; I felt inexplicably exhilarated. I decided to take it home with me so I could check it out and try to understand its meaning. I knew it held some sort of magic within it.

I reluctantly set the mirror on the bed with the books to free my arms of its cumbersome weight. The tiny one room cabin held more than I'd expected. How could so many amazing things be in one small space? I noticed a shelf on the wall with a variety of vials. Many of the labels were made illegible by the hands of time, but I was able to decipher a few. "Eye of Newt," "Mandrake Root," and "Mermaid Hair" stood out to me. They seemed to call my name. I grabbed them and set them on the bed too. Midnight purred and looked intently into my eyes.

The more time I spent in the cabin, the less menacing it seemed. *I don't think this place is filled with evil. I think it's filled with sorrow.* The thought struck me as I inspected an old doll. It sat in one corner of the room, its porcelain face covered in so much dust that I couldn't make out its eyes. It reminded me of something Jenni would like to play with. For a few moments, I considered dragging the thing home with me to give to her, but it was so grimy I worried it would fall apart.

My stomach growled. How long had it been since breakfast? I had no clue, and I hadn't bothered to bring a watch or my phone with me. I knew I should probably head home. I gathered the items I'd collected from the bed, treating each artifact with care. For some reason, I didn't feel ready to leave. Something kept me there in that room; my feet were unwilling to leave until the right moment.

It was then that I noticed a rolled-up piece of thin, worn-out parchment. Upon inspection, I realized it was a map: a tired, torn map of a three-hundred-year-old Tansy. I grabbed it to take home with me

I crept back out of the cabin, Midnight underfoot, and stopped in the doorway. I looked back over the space. It was creepy, but a marvelous magic made its home there. Good and evil commingled here, twisting and tangling together through the centuries. The good in this place seemed to be fighting against the forces of evil I'd noticed when I first arrived. I knew I would return to this place. I was inexplicably pulled to the cabin—to its story, and to its former occupant.

The ghosts thought that Lavina had cursed them, but my heart told me she wasn't a bad person. I felt tied to this witchy woman who died centuries before I was born. As unlikely as it was, a bond with the witch who died so long ago began to form in my heart.

Sunlight assaulted my eyes as I left the dark cabin, breaking the spell of the past and snapping me into the reality that lay before me.

A DISCOVERY

As I trekked through Tansy, I began to wish I'd brought a backpack. The weight of my assortment of items from the cabin strained my arms. Holding all the creepy treasures felt awkward. Stacked into a jumbling tower, they blocked much of my face.

I noticed some strange looks from my living neighbors. Mrs. Baker, who lived down the street from me, stopped in the middle of the sidewalk and looked me up and down, her mouth wide, and shook her head at me. I was used to this, of course. I am something of an oddball, an outsider, and "a tad bit off," as my sixth-grade teacher, Mrs. Bern, often observed. It was hard for me to ignore the spirits surrounding me, making me appear to be an awkward daydreamer or like I talked to myself. A lot of people thought I was a freak.

I grumbled under my breath, and my stomach growled as I ungracefully meandered through town. I was just three blocks from home when I rounded a corner to find a group of kids from my school huddled by the sweet shop. Desperate to keep them in the dark about my creepy collection from the witch's cabin, my stomach panged with dread when, much to my dismay, I spotted Tara Gleason among the crowd.

I considered taking another way home, but it was too late. Tara saw me and all of the items from Lavina's. She turned toward Holly

Penterbrook and snickered. "Look," she said, "it's Gross Grace! I wonder what the weirdo has been up to?"

"What. A. Freak." Holly made a point to extend each syllable as she spoke.

"Hey, Grace!" Tara said in a sugary sweet voice usually reserved for puppies.

"Hi." I looked at my feet and tried to pick up the pace. *Why is that terrible girl everywhere I go?* I wondered, hoping our interaction would be brief.

"What'cha got there, Gracie?" Tara taunted.

"Nothing. Just some of my grandma's things." I lied, still looking at my feet.

Tara tried to grab the map off the top of the pile, but I jumped back just in time. As I did, Bain Bello walked out of the bakery next door with a bulging bag of baked goods. He watched what was happening and stepped between Tara and me.

"What's going on, Tara?" Bain said, his brown eyes on me.

"Nothing, Bain. Not your business," Tara responded.

"It's my business when you decide to bother my friend Grace." His gaze never left my face.

Friend? Since when are we friends? My cheeks reddened.

"Whatever. You're both weird," Tara said as she turned south and walked away from us, Holly following behind her like a ducking tailing its mother.

"Thanks, Bain."

"No problem." He smiled back at me, staring a moment longer than necessary. His eyes wandered to the items I carried. My mind filled with fear. I didn't want anyone—not even Bain—to see what I had.

"Want some help carrying all of that?" he asked, his hands reaching toward my overflowing arms as he spoke.

"Nope. I'm fine. Thanks, though." I turned my bundle of magical items away from him, and as I did, I accidentally bumped his hand. A warm, tingling sensation filled my arm where we'd touched. I felt myself blushing again.

With that, I took off in the direction of my house on Willow Way, my sneakers slapping the pavement as I sprinted away from Bain. My mind teemed with thoughts of witches, ghosts, bullies, and a cute boy.

I soon spied my violet Victorian home across the alley, relieved that I'd almost made it. I was just about to head inside when I noticed my dad sitting on the purple porch swing, reading the newspaper in the sunshine. I knew I couldn't let him see my witchy treasures. He'd ask too many questions. Slouching down behind Mrs. Baker's mailbox, I contemplated what to do next.

What is he doing home this time of day? I wondered.

I tried to make myself minuscule. I hoped that my shirt color would camouflage with the gray mailbox. I attempted to appear invisible, slipping into the shadows, barely breathing. Silently pleading with my father to leave the porch, I closed my eyes for a moment while I tried to decide my next move. My wishes seemed to weave a basket of protection over me. A car passed, and Dad looked up to wave to the driver. Though he was looking right at me after the car drove away, I somehow went unnoticed. After a few moments, he silently rose and entered the house, his eyes glazed over.

I let out a grateful gasp and bounded toward the backyard in search of a spot to safely stash all the items I'd collected. I opened the heavy iron gate, the scent of roses wafting to my nose as I entered the large, fenced yard. My eyes darted around the space, hopping from the overflowing garden beds my mom meticulously kept, to the towering maple tree in the center of the yard, past the worn hammock my dad loved. None of these spots would do. My eyes stopped on the old shed standing in one corner of the yard. My parents almost never used the rickety old building. I knew my secrets would be safe within its weak walls.

Stepping inside, I moved aside boxes until I found one labeled "Christmas Decorations." It was June. The box wouldn't be needed for many months. I carefully stowed my treasures in the box and stacked several others on top of it, just to be safe.

A twinge of sorrow pulsed through me upon being separated from my new collection. The books begged to be read. I wanted to hold the handle of the heavy mirror. My desire to examine the map and see what the streets of Tansy looked like long ago was immense. The vials seemed to call to me. But for now, I needed to go inside and eat my late lunch.

One salami sandwich later, I realized that my evening wouldn't be spent surrounded by maps and books. My parents made plans to celebrate my report card. Dad took half a day off for a dentist appointment and wouldn't be returning to the bank.

"I rented that movie you've been going on about. The one with the ghosts? I thought I'd make us some popcorn and we could watch it. Then when your mom gets off work, we want to take you to dinner to celebrate your good grades."

"Thanks, Dad." I tried not to let my disappointment show. Normally, I'd love to watch a movie with him—especially a ghost story, which he usually shunned. But I really wanted to spend some time with the collection I'd brought back from Lavina's cabin.

Cozying up on the sofa, I tried unsuccessfully to pay attention to the movie. I could think only of the curse, and everything—the sound of Dad crunching popcorn, the clock ticking on the wall, the movie itself—distracted me. I had no clue what happened in the film, but I don't think Dad noticed.

We met Mom at Tansy's only restaurant after she got home from working as a nurse at the hospital in Luna. I loved the flawless French cafe. Unfortunately, my mind drifted elsewhere. I chatted with my parents and ate delicious baked Camembert, but I thought only of solving the mystery that cursed my ghoulish friends.

After picking at a slice of caramel cake, I headed home with my parents. I thanked them for a wonderful day and headed to bed. I set my alarm clock for 3:00 a.m. when I knew they'd be asleep. I was excited to head back to the shed to inspect the items I'd gathered, so sleep evaded me for quite some time. Eventually, however, I slipped into a dreamless sleep.

Several hours later, flashlight in hand, I made a beeline for the "Christmas Decorations" box and removed the the lid. I removed the three books, the map, and the mirror and let out a breath I didn't realize I'd been holding in for far too long. I removed the three books, the map, and the mirror.

I tried to get cozy on a discarded couch and spread the items out in front of me, trying to decide which to inspect first. Midnight meowed and floated up next to me on the sofa.

"Hey, little kitty," I said.

He meowed again and sat next to the map.

"Should I check out this map first?"

Looking straight into my eyes, he meowed again. I'd always believed that Midnight understood more than your average cat, but this was getting kind of weird.

"Okay, map it is," I told him.

I gazed at the map for several minutes. It was alluring, with its hand-drawn notes scrawled next to points of interest in an immaculate swirling script. All of the notes were written in poetic rhymes.

Just outside the walls of the town of Tansy, the witch's cabin was marked. It was drawn as it must have looked three hundred years before, cheery and surrounded by beautiful flowers. Next to it were the words:

Here be Lavina, White Witch of the Wood
Come from far or near with whatever ails you
This witch will heal with magic so good
And you'll part ways feeling anew.

"The White Witch of the Wood," I whispered. "She saw herself as a healer. Would she really curse the town?" I thought back to my time in the cabin, how the more I'd learned about Lavina, the less scary she seemed. I was starting to feel the White Witch of the Wood was nothing like the evil witches I'd read about in storybooks.

Midnight hopped onto my lap and purred. I shone my flashlight onto the moth-eaten map. Next to the field in which I'd met with the spirits the day before read:

If for potion making you seek
eye of newt or the sacred berry,
in this field shall you peek
and away you'll walk with all you can carry.

I wondered exactly what was meant by "the sacred berry" and if they still grew in the field. My eyes darted around the page, past the bank, beyond the post office, and landed on the other side of the city, then I gasped. My house was marked on the map. Next to it read:

If magical companions you do lack,
come to this home and head on in,
for every Friday when the sky goes black
it is the home of the White Magic Coven.

My head swirled, and my palms began to sweat. Three hundred years before, my home had been a meeting place for witches. In the dining room where I'd taken my first steps, witches gathered in secret. In the yard where I'd swung from the weeping willow tree, witches may have sat around a fire and swapped spells. Could pieces of white magic have been left behind?

"Midnight, did you know? Did you know this was a home to witches?" I asked the little black ghost cat, not expecting an answer.

Midnight meowed, and maybe it was a trick of the light, but I could have sworn that he nodded his shadowy head.

MAGIC IN MY BLOOD

"It wasn't ours to tell. It was yours to discover," Thomas said softly.

It was less than twenty-four hours after I visited Lavina's cabin. So much had changed in a day. I sat on my bed, Midnight next to my feet and Polly and Thomas floating above me, looking down at me with pained expressions.

I brushed a raven curl of hair away from my eyes. A lump formed in my throat as I fought back tears and looked up at my two closest spirit friends. They'd *known*. They'd known all along, and they'd never told me that my home was a safe-house for witches. Never hinted at its history. Never helped me to learn of its lineage. It was more than that, however. The house had been in my family for generations. This home, built as a sanctuary for sorceresses, a haven for hexes, a preserve for potions, had only housed members of my mom's family. And if they were witches, what did that mean for me?

Was magic something you learned? A skill? Or was it something passed on to you from your family, like freckles or long fingers? Was magic hereditary? I wanted to ask my friends if they knew. I couldn't formulate the question. It hung in the air, just waiting to be knocked down by the first to speak.

It would explain so much if I had magical powers. My connection with spirits. My tendency to will myself to go unseen like I had with my dad the day before. It would explain my inability to connect with the living. My life would make more sense if, perhaps, I *was* a witch.

Finally, I let out a breath and tried to form the question building in my mind. "Am I...does this mean...um...is magic something I could have...inherited?" I bumbled, unable to express myself.

Thomas and Polly grinned at me. Midnight mewed.

"You, my dear," Thomas began, "are filled with magic. Generations of magical people have lived in this house, and none of them came close to your power."

"Generations of witches? So..." I paused, taking a big breath. "Grandma? Mom? Are they magic?"

"Oh yes," said Polly. "I remember your mother as a little girl. I'd watch her play in the garden. All of the animals assembled whenever she was near. Bugs, bunnies, deer, birds, and butterflies surrounded her as she sat in the swing. She possessed such a strong bond with nature, but, the older she got, the more she moved away from her magic. I doubt she ever truly understood what she was doing."

"And your grandmother!" Thomas exclaimed. "She practiced magic before your mother's birth. She mixed potions for everything imaginable."

I could picture my eccentric grandma doing just that. The more I thought about it, the less of a stretch it was to imagine magic running through my veins.

Thomas continued. "There was still a small gathering of magical people who met here in those days. But when your grandmother laid eyes on her little daughter for the first time, she swore she'd stop her spells. The coven quit meeting here after that."

"Why would having a daughter make her want to give up magic?"

Polly's face lost its happy expression. Thomas floated down to my bed to look me in the eye. I had a hard time making myself meet his gaze.

"Tansy is a wonderful town, but we have a history of not being understanding of people who are different."

"Well that's an understatement," I said, thinking of the kids in school.

Thomas nodded. "For generations, there have been people who distrust those who use magic. It was not just Lavina who was driven away or excluded by the people of this town. I am ashamed to say that like your family passed magic down to you, other families in this town have passed down hatred for generations. Your grandmother wanted to protect her little girl from the people of Tansy. So your mother never knew what she was. And you, my dear Grace, have not known what *you* are. Until today."

I tried to take all of that in, but my mind kept coming back to the fact that my friends and family kept my true identity a secret from me. My body grew hot, and my shoulders tensed.

"So, you knew. You knew that I was different for a reason. That no living person other than my parents liked me for a reason. Everyone around me knew something I knew nothing of."

Polly's permanently preteen face looked as if I'd slapped her.

"We didn't want to hurt you. We know it's not easy for you, being the only one around who can see us."

I sighed. "I just need to be alone with my thoughts for a while."

"Grace, please. Please understand that we care about you. We talked it over years ago when you were still a toddler. We knew that your grandmother had only been trying to protect your family. We decided that if you figured it out on your own, we would tell you the truth. But, as a group, we decided it wasn't our place to go against your grandmother's wishes. And now that you've found your magic, we will do what we can for you. But we didn't practice magic when we were living. We've watched the women of Willow Way for centuries, but we never had the gifts that you have," Thomas replied, his tone even.

Gifts. Magic. Witchcraft. This was all too much for me. I was already weird. Now I was a witch? I didn't know if I should be delighted or devastated. Having magical powers could have its advantages for sure. But if what Thomas had told me was true, witches weren't exactly given celebratory parties in these parts. Isn't that why Lavina left in the first place? Why Grandma had hidden her magic?

"Thank you, Thomas. Thank you, Polly. I need to process this," I told them from underneath the quilt.

"We understand, Grace. But know this, if anyone can break the curse, it's you, wee witch," Thomas said.

In an instant, they left, and I was alone with only Midnight and my thoughts. I had many of them. My mind spun in tornadic circles, until, exhaustion overtook me, and I drifted off to sleep. I stayed hidden still under the quilt as if it could protect me from the changes that were imminent.

A DREAM

I tossed and turned as I slept. I slipped into an anxious state of dreaming. It was dark, the sky an inky black. The only light came from a flickering fire. I stood inches from the hot flames. A heavy black cauldron sat on the fire. A circle of marching witches surrounded me. I stood at their center as they chanted and chattered and cawed and cackled. They looked like the witches of cartoons: green skin; warts on their noses; tall, pointed black hats; many of them carried old-fashioned broomsticks. My stomach lurched with fear.

"Join us!" called one.

"Drink up!" demanded another, holding out a silver goblet of gurgling green goo mere inches from my face.

I turned round and round, trying to find a way out of the circle. There was no path for escape. Everywhere I turned, a witch popped up to block my way. Everything spun in a dizzying frenzy.

"You can't fight your destiny, Grace. You are a witch, and you can't deny it!" screeched a sorceress as she pointed a slender green finger at me.

"Join us! Join us!" chanted the crowd in loud, scratchy voices.

I fell to the ground. I grabbed at my ears, trying to block the groans and growls of the wall of witches. They started to close in on me, inching closer and closer as I sobbed into the soil. Hands began to grope and grab at me, pulling my arms and legs from every direction.

A scream escaped my throat as terror overtook me. As I cried, the cartoonish witches disappeared, and I found myself sitting on the steps of my grandma's porch in Luna on a sunny afternoon.

The door to the house squeaked open, footsteps followed and, in a moment, Grandma Gertrude sat down beside me.

"What's wrong, Gracie Bug? Are you scared?" she asked, putting her arm around my shoulders.

"I am," I whispered, hardly able to get the words out.

"Why?"

"Because, Grandma, it's totally terrifying. I thought I knew who I was. But I don't. I don't know at all!" I told her between sobs.

"But you have always known." My grandma's tone was even and sweet.

"I haven't! You never told me! You could have told me!"

"Think about it, Grace. It's always been there. Inside of you. You have such magnificent magic, my dear. You can't hide it, not even from yourself."

"But Grandma," I began, but she cut me off.

"Always. It's always been there. It's as much a part of you as your black hair and gray eyes. Think about all the times you've managed to maneuver through a crowd unseen. The times bullies chased you, and you seemed to become invisible. Your magic is strong, Grace, and it's not going away."

Grandma Gertrude stood, holding her wrinkled right hand out to me. I took it and stood up, then I wrapped my arms around my grandma, leaned into her green blouse, and sobbed silently for several minutes.

"What do I do next, Grandma?"

"You wake up and come see me," she said. "I'll be waiting for you."

And with that, I woke up, at home in my bed, sweaty and scared. I waited for a few moments, thinking about the dream and its meaning. The first half of the dream, I perceived to be a nightmare, a horrible nightmare, but something made-up. The portion on

Grandma's porch felt as real as any of my memories. Could Grandma have actually been speaking with me as I slept? Such an idea would have been crazy only forty-eight hours ago. But so much had changed.

I got out of bed and went downstairs, found my mom, and said, "I need to visit Grandma. Now."

TO GRANDMOTHER'S HOUSE WE GO

It took a few minutes for me to convince my mom to drive me to my grandma's house, but soon, we got into the car and headed to Luna. Mom failed to fathom just why I had to go to my grandma's at exactly that moment, but she realized how desperate I was, so she drove me.

The twenty-minute drive was filled with mountain vistas and awkward silence as Mom tried to figure out what was going on with me, and I thought over what I might say to my grandma.

Grandma Gertrude was waiting on the porch when we pulled into the driveway. She wore the same green blouse from my dream. When I saw this, my heart beat faster, and everything swirled in a wave of dizziness. Had the dream actually been real?

Grandma stood and walked directly to me. "I was expecting you." She turned to my mom. "Hello, Gabby. Grace and I need to take a little walk and have a chat. Why don't you go see how Dad is doing?"

Mom's brow furrowed, but she agreed and went inside. As the door closed behind her, Grandma took my hand in her own.

"How are you, dear? I'm glad you could make it out here so soon after your vision."

"Vision?" I asked, my mouth hanging open in confusion.

"Your nightmare, I suppose you would call it."

I shook my head in disbelief. "You mean it was real?"

"I am not sure 'real' is the right word. The beginning of it was simply a bad dream. It was a compilation of everything you thought you knew about magic. Cartoons and picture books give our history a bad reputation. You're going to have to learn to forget what you know, and know what you encounter."

My head was spinning, but I nodded, encouraging Grandma to say more.

"The part where you and I had a chat here on the porch, however, was a shared experience. You were able to channel me while you slept."

I tried to guess what Grandma meant, but, overwhelmed, I couldn't comprehend it. Grandma stepped in toward me, took my hand, and said, "Let's walk."

We ambled through the garden gate and into the grassy field that bordered Grandma's yard. We were enveloped by sunshine and the sweet, earthy smell of nature. Bees buzzed by, fawns frolicked, and rabbits dashed through the field as we walked. Normally, I loved the wildlife at Grandma's, but not that day. All I could think of was getting the answers I needed.

"Please don't be angry with me, Grace," Grandma said, her voice strained.

"I'm not angry, Grandma, just confused."

"It's a lot to take in, especially when you consider how you were raised. Your mother won't believe in magic, no matter how powerful she may be. It's my fault, I suppose. I tried to hide it from her when she was a child. I'd been harassed for practicing magic, and I didn't want that for her. A child should not have to worry about such things, or so I thought, but losing such a big part of who you truly are? That's worse than standing up for yourself any day."

Grandma's face displayed the decades of devastation she'd endured. I'd never seen this sadness in my grandma's eyes before. A tear streamed down her wrinkled cheek as she spoke.

"My deepest regret in my life is masking your mother's magic. She could have been magnificent. Oh, the way animals responded to her as a child!" Grandma waved her hands in the air as she spoke.

"But I never guided her with her gifts. I never told her who she really was. I'd occasionally mix a potion to weaken her power and slip it into her juice."

I tried not to let my shock show on my face. Looking down, I smoothed out an imaginary wrinkle on my shirt.

"If she mentioned anything about her skills, I'd chastise her and tell her it was all in her head. And soon enough, that special light in her began to fade. If you don't water your wisteria, it will wilt, and if you don't cultivate your gifts, you'll be left without any magical capability."

"So, is that why she's so against anything that's just a little bit different?" I asked, thinking of all the times I'd tried to tell Mom about the many ghosts of Tansy only to be dismissed.

Grandma sniffled and nodded. "It's all my fault." A deep, guttural sob escaped her wrinkled lips.

Grandma had always been larger than life. Not in size, but demeanor. In that moment, however, for the first time in my life, my grandma looked small to me. Her hunched shoulders, drooping head, and crossed arms all worked together to shrink the woman I'd always seen as Wonder Woman. "Grandma, you were only trying to protect her." I wrapped my arms around her.

"It wasn't right. It wasn't mine to take from her. But I am not going to make that mistake with you. I am so sorry that this all comes as such a shock to you, Gracie. I knew from the day you were born that you held a deep power. White magic vibrates from your very soul. I've spent the last twelve years debating about when to tell you. Until you conjured me in that vision, I had no clue that you knew."

"I just figured it out. I knew I was different. But I didn't know it was magic. Not until I found the map and saw—"

"Map?" Grandma cut me off. "What map?"

"From Lavina's cabin—"

"Lavina? You mean the White Witch of the Wood?"

I nodded.

"But how did you even know to go there?"

I told Grandma everything. I started with the ghosts who were always there and how no living person ever accepted my ability to see spirits. Then, about Midnight and how he never left my side. I confessed about the gathering of ghouls in my bedroom the day before, and how they begged for my assistance in breaking the curse. I told her how I'd gone to the cabin and found the items that seemed to speak my name, and how, upon my return, I'd hidden from my father in plain sight. Finally, I explained how, when I'd seen the map and the house marked as a coven, I knew in my heart something that had always been in the back of my mind, and that the ghosts had confirmed it for me.

Grandma stood silent for several seconds, rendered speechless by the story. She took me by the hand, turned toward the house, and said, "We've got some work to do."

We walked toward the house for about a minute, then Grandma stopped short, her feet seemingly turned to bricks. Sweat beaded on her forehead. Her breathing became labored.

"Grandma? Are you okay?"

Grandma nodded, then she spoke. "It's time. We have to tell your mother who we are. Who she truly is. We cannot be a family of secrets and lies any longer."

My eyes widened. Could my mom handle this news? Mom, who didn't like anything outside of the norm. I worried about her reaction upon learning that she, herself, was far from normal. I wasn't sure what she would do.

"It's going to be alright, Grace. Let's go inside and face the music."

MY MOM LEVITATES

Grandma Gertrude was a woman of action, not the type to have long discussions when a simple maneuver would do the trick. She marched up the steps of the front porch and threw open the door with her mind. I trailed behind her, eyes wide. She walked into the room where Mom and Grandpa Steve sat on the sofa and waved her hand to draw open all of the drapes. To further prove her point, Grandma waved her hand again and made Mom levitate a few inches off the ground. Mom gasped, her eyes bulging. Grandpa raised one eyebrow but said nothing, a knowing look coming over his wrinkled face.

Grandma released Mom, who fell back onto the sofa, mouth agape, and the color drained from her face.

"It's time we talked," Grandma said.

Mom sat pale and motionless for a full minute. The only sound in the room was her rapid breath. Grandpa opened his mouth, but Grandma held up a finger as if to say, *give her a moment.*

After several minutes, Grandma placed a hand on Mom's shoulder and said, "Sweetie? Are you ready?"

Mom didn't speak, but she nodded slightly.

"For many generations, as far back as our family has lived in the shadow of the Fantasma Mountains, we've had certain..." she paused, seeming to search for the right word, "abilities."

"As in the ability to lift people without touching them?" Mom's words snapped out of her mouth in an almost hysterical tone. She dug her fingers into the arm of the sofa as if holding on for dear life.

"Like that. Among other things. It's been different for every member of the family. And the others who are like us."

"Others?" Mom said, staring at her hands as she wrung them on her lap.

"Yes, there have been magical people in and around Tansy since its founding. But, as you know, the people in Tansy have never liked anything that seems different. So, we learned to hide our abilities. Around the time you were born, there was a lot of talk about the 'weirdos' and wanting to drive them out of town. I didn't want anyone to ever hurt you, so I hid my magic. And yours."

Mom looked up, eyes wide. "My magic?"

"Yes. Your magic. You could have been great, if it wasn't for me," Grandma told her, taking Mom's hand in her own, tears running down her cheeks.

An hour later, Mom was up to speed. Grandma explained as much as she could, answered any question Mom had, and tried to keep everyone calm. Severely shaken, confused, and her feelings understandably hurt, I watched as Mom struggled to comprehend the situation. She sat on the couch, her gray eyes misty and her breath rattling, staring at her brown sandals as if they held the answers she needed. After several minutes, she looked up at Grandma and said, "I forgive you."

"Oh," Grandma sobbed, wiping tears from her eyes, "Thank you. Thank you."

Mom sniffled, then turned her focus to me. "I want to help you, too, Gracie. It sounds like you have quite the situation on your hands. I don't know anything about magic, and I can't just walk out of work, but I will do what I can."

Grandma spoke up then, revealing another problem for us to

tackle. "Even in the world of magic, the ability to speak to spirits is quite rare. I have never met anyone who possessed this power in my entire life," she said, her brow furrowed. "I am unable to guide you through this particular gifting."

It figures that I am still the weird one, even when it comes to magic, I thought, sinking deeper into the cushy sofa.

The next problem was one of practicality. No one knew what the next step was. The ghosts suspected Lavina cursed them, but they had no way to know which curse she'd used. Breaking a known curse can be done, but Grandma explained that it's nearly impossible to fix a spell that you can't identify.

"Grace, my dear, you need to ready yourself for research. You'll have to read every one of those books you brought back from the White Witch's cabin."

SINCE THIS WAS all new to Mom and me, Grandma planned white magic lessons for both of us. Grandma insisted the first lesson happen before we went home that evening even though Mom was still in shock. She wanted to be there for me and the spirits of Tansy, but she had a lot to sort through on her own. Mom wanted to see if she could get some of her magic back after so many years, and Grandma seemed to think it was possible. Grandpa, as it turned out, didn't process any magical ability. He couldn't offer more than moral support.

The feeling I had as I waited for my lesson to begin was half Christmas morning and half test anxiety. My stomach lurched as I waited for Grandma to start. She set a small silver spoon on the side table.

"Move it," she instructed.

Mom walked toward the table, reaching for the spoon with her left hand.

Grandma shook her head. Her gray eyes sparkled as her face curled up with a small smile. "With your mind, dear."

"Oh!" Mom's face reddened, and her shoulders slumped. "I'm not sure how."

"And you never will be if you don't try," Grandma told her.

I'd never seen my mother look quite this uncomfortable. Her face twisted into a look of panic. After a few moments, Mom glared at the spoon, appearing to believe that rage was the key to working her magic. The silver spoon stayed still.

"You have to believe the spoon will move, sweetheart," Grandma said, setting her hand on Mom's tense shoulder.

"I don't think I'm there yet. Gracie, why don't you try?"

I looked up at my mom and took note of her misty eyes and flushed cheeks. I didn't realize how hard this would be for her. I turned to Grandma to see what she thought I should do next.

Grandma looked as if she might object. She opened her thin lips, then closed them again, and nodded at me.

I looked at the spoon. I thought about everything that had happened over the past two days. The image of Grandma picking up Mom with her mind flashed through my head. *If Grandma can pick up Mom, I can move that spoon,* I thought. The spoon shook slightly. It was a small movement, but it was clear to everyone in the room that it happened.

Grandma cheered. Mom threw her arms around me. I looked at the spoon in disbelief.

"I really am magical, aren't I?" I said quietly.

"Yes, dear. You really, truly are," Grandma replied, her voice thick with pride.

"Life is never going to be the same again," I whispered.

Mom brushed her hand against my cheek. "I think you're right," she whispered back.

After a quick dinner (sorceresses or not, grandmothers can't let their grandchildren go home on empty stomachs), Mom and I headed back to Tansy. I needed to get back to the shed to see what I could find out from the items I'd brought back from Lavina's cabin.

The drive back to Tansy was quiet. A few blocks from the house, I glanced over at Mom. She looked as white as a sheet.

"Are you okay, Mom?" I asked timidly.

"I will be. I keep reliving moments of my childhood. Moments where I *knew* I was special. It makes me wonder how different things would have been if Grandma hadn't been so afraid. For me and for you. Because I saw in you what I saw in myself as a child. And I am so, so sorry, sweetheart. I shut you down every time you tried to tell me what was happening with you. But that's over. We're going to figure out all of this white magic stuff together, okay?" Tears streamed down Mom's cheeks.

"Okay, Mom." I took her hand in my own, and we finished the ride in comfortable silence.

10 INVESTIGATION

Dad was sitting on the porch when we pulled up into our dirt driveway, dust stirring up from the ground in brown clouds. I looked at Mom's blotchy, red face, puffy eyes, and tear-stained cheeks and knew we were going to have to tell my dad. My heartbeat picked up a bit.

"What do we say to him?" I asked.

Mom turned to look at me as she opened the car door. "We tell him the truth, even if it's hard. We don't need any more secrets in this family." She slipped out of the car and walked right up to my father, her head held high.

I scrambled out of the car, trailing behind her. A few ghosts swirled around where he sat on the porch, but I shook my head at them, letting them know it wasn't a good time to talk. They disappeared as I climbed the steps.

"Gabby, what's wrong?" Concern washed over Dad's face as he reached his hand out to Mom, brushing her cheek with his hand.

"Honey, there's something we have to tell you, but we better sit down for this." Mom gestured to the small wicker table that sat on the other end of the large, wrap-around porch. The space between where we stood and that little table was filled with tension. We walked our way through it like you'd walk through mud, one heavy step at a time.

My stomach churned as I pulled a chair out and sat. I looked down at the birds on the patterned seat cushion, wishing I had their wings to fly my way out of this conversation. The sound of younger kids playing nearby filled the air, their happy chatter in harsh contrast with our awkward silence.

"Okay, you're freaking me out here. What's going on?" Dad asked, his voice cracking a bit.

Mom took a deep breath, pushed a piece of her chestnut hair out of her face, and spoke. "There's no easy way to say this, so I am just going to be blunt." She swallowed, seemingly unable to make the next part come out.

"What is it? Are you sick?"

"No. It's nothing like that. Honey, Grace and I just came from my mother's. It seems that...we...we have magic powers," Mom sputtered.

Dad stared at her for a moment, then burst into laughter. "You really had me going there for a second. It's mean to scare your husband!" He poked her playfully.

"Dad. She's not kidding," I said quietly.

"Oh, come on, Grace."

"She's right, dear. I am trying to tell you something," Mom said, her voice a bit more confident than before. "For generations, the members of my mom's family have all held magic abilities. My mom moved me with her mind tonight. I have a special way with animals. And Grace..."

"I speak to the dead," I said. "I always have."

"You what?" Dad asked in a sharp tone, fixing his blue eyes fixed on me.

"The dead. I talk to them. I see them. I'm friends with them."

"Your friends...are ghosts?"

"Most of them, yes."

Dad shook his head, leaned back, and covered his eyes with his hand. He was silent for a long moment. He moved his hand, then shifted his gaze back on my mom.

"Your mother moved you with her mind? Gertrude picked you up...with only her mind?"

"Yes, sweetie. I know it's crazy. But Mom says our people have been able to do unusual things as long as they've lived in Tansy." Mom paused, then looked right into his eyes. "Magical things."

Dad looked as washed out as one of my ghosts. I put my hand on his. "You okay?"

He didn't speak, nor move. Catatonic, he stared into space, his rapid breathing the only sign of life.

"Why don't you let me talk to him, Grace?" Mom said.

Nodding, I pushed back my chair and stood. I rested my hand briefly on Dad's shoulder, then walked toward the backyard. Midnight waited for me next to the shed.

"Hello, Midnight."

"Meow," he responded.

I opened the door to the shed and headed toward the box of Christmas decorations. Before I could even open it, Polly appeared.

"Are you still mad?" Polly asked.

"No. I get why you didn't say anything about my family's history with magic. I wish I'd known, but I can't stay mad at you."

"Good. I'm here to help however I can."

"What can you tell me about Lavina?" I asked, hoping Polly could shed some light on the conflicting views of Lavina I'd been presented with.

"Not a lot. I wasn't born for twenty years after she'd left the town of Tansy. But I can tell you what the others have told me. None of the spirits lived before Lavina's time. Those who've been here the longest all died right after she was banished. Apparently, the townspeople were terrible to her. I think Thomas might be able to tell you more. He died two weeks after Lavina left. He's been here longer than anyone else."

"That must have been so hard for him," I said, thinking about what the afterlife must have been for Thomas, for all the ghosts, knowing that something waited for them on the other side, but being held back by a curse.

I opened the box and pulled out a book. Flipping through it aimlessly, I passed pages upon pages of potions: potions to make your hair grow faster, potions to heal a broken heart, potions to make a garden grow faster. None seemed like what one could use to trap spirits in one place for eternity.

I set the book down and picked up another. Hours passed as I paged through the books, occasionally chatting with Polly about a potion or with Midnight about a bit of magic, but, eventually, it got late, and I was too tired to continue my work. I made myself a promise to get right back to it in the morning.

Feeling defeated, I headed into the house, wondering as I walked if I would be able to complete what seemed such an impossible task, even with Grandma and Mom helping out. Even with the ghosts attempting to assist me, and Midnight meowing beside me, I felt helpless and incapable of doing what I'd been asked.

As I made my way through the backyard, Jenni appeared. A smile spread across my face. She'd always been able to cheer me up. The ghosts had all told me that she used to play peekaboo with me to stop my tears when I was a baby, something she'd learned taking care of her baby brother before she died. These days, however, I found our roles reversed. Jenni was six forever. She needed me more than I needed her.

"Are you mad at me? 'Cause I heard you were mad at Polly and Thomas about not telling you about the magic stuff." Jenni looked at her feet as she spoke. "I really don't know about magic, and all the grown-up ghosts said I shouldn't tell."

"No. I'm not mad. Don't worry about it, Jenni."

"Okay. I love you, Gracie. I would be so totally sad if you were mad at me."

"I love you, too. I've got to get inside. We'll talk soon, okay?"

"Okay!" Jenni said, then disappeared.

A high pitch sound whistled in the kitchen, where I found Dad holding the cheery yellow teapot. He held the pot out to me and nodded to two cups sitting on the counter.

"Hey, kiddo. Mom filled me in a bit better. Sorry I wasn't really responsive before. How are you doing with all of this?"

"I'm overwhelmed, Dad," I admitted, my voice cracking.

The color drained from Dad's face. It struck me then just how much this was for him to take in, too. His wife and daughter were witches. *Witches!* He'd been living a happy life in a tiny town working as a teller at a bank and now...his house was full of witches. It seemed absolutely absurd.

"Well, Gracie, I have to admit, I'm overwhelmed too. But I know you, and I know your mom and grandma, and you are the three most amazing women I've ever met. It shouldn't surprise me that you three have magical abilities. You're all too special to be mere mortals." He smiled and pulled me in for an enormous hug.

I hugged him back, holding as tightly as I could muster, the familiar scent of his driftwood aftershave filling the space between us. When he finally released me, we were both a little teary-eyed. Things were not going to be the same in the house on Willow Way anymore.

It was much later than either of us typically went to bed, but we talked and had tea and enjoyed time together. As I stood to go to bed, Dad promised to go out to Lavina's cabin with me the next day.

"I may not have special abilities, but I do have a great eye for detail. Maybe we'll find something you missed before."

"Thanks, Dad," I replied. "If nothing else, it would be nice to have your company out there. It's a bit creepy in that cabin."

I was so overcome with a feeling of exhaustion that I had to will myself to walk up the creaky stairs of my old house. When I got to my room, Thomas was waiting for me, floating over my desk. In spite of the fact that spirits surrounded me every day, his unexpected presence startled me. I stumbled over my own feet and let out a yelp of surprise.

"Sorry, Grace. I didn't mean to scare you. I just wanted to talk to you before you went to bed. Did you find anything?" Thomas asked.

I exhaled a wistful sigh and shook my head. "I'm sorry. I'm trying, but it might take some time to sort through it all."

He smiled. "Don't be sad. I've been waiting three hundred years. At least now, I have hope."

"But what if you keep fading? I don't want you to..." I couldn't force myself to finish.

"Then you'll save the others," Thomas said, his eyes watery.

And with that, he left, and I was alone with my thoughts and worries.

THE VOICE

Morning arrived before I even realized I'd slept. Warm sunlight flickered upon my eyes. I groaned and rolled over, but as soon as I started to move, a voice startled me.

"Try the mirror," the voice demanded.

"The what?" I yawned and opened my eyes.

"The mirror!" the voice ordered.

I looked around, trying to locate the source of the bossy voice. I couldn't see anyone.

"Um. Hello?" I said, confused.

There was no reply. *What on Earth is going on?* I wondered. *Was that a dream? Are there ghosts I can't see? Am I going insane? I don't need to go crazy right now. I've got enough to deal with!*

I didn't have much time to wonder about the source of the voice, because a knock at the door pulled me away from my thoughts.

"Time to get up, buttercup!" called Dad from the hallway. "We've got a cabin to explore!"

"Okay, Dad!" I called, still looking around the room, feeling befuddled. I hopped out of bed and started looking in unlikely locations for the source of the now-absent voice. I got down on my hands and knees and peeked under the bed. There was no one there. Not a soul was found in my closet. No haunt hid on my windowsill. No apparitions hid near the huddle of art supplies on my desk. I felt slightly silly, crawling around my room looking for an unseen speaker, but I didn't know what else to do. After several minutes, I gave up on the search. I tossed on my bath robe, and left the room, looking over my shoulder one last time.

I headed down the stairs and into the kitchen to eat breakfast. My parents sat at the white wooden dining table, eating waffles with whipped cream.

"Do you want some waffles?" Mom asked.

"Sure," I replied, still distracted by the voice I hoped wasn't in my head.

Mom got up and prepared a plate for me. "Whipped cream? Berries? Syrup?"

"Okay," I replied grimly.

"Is there a problem, Gracie? You usually love waffles. It's kind of why I made them. Don't tell me you're going to be one of those teenagers who doesn't eat because it's really unhealthy—"

I cut her off. "No, no. Waffles are fine. Great, even. I'm sorry. I'm distracted this morning."

And I had every reason to be distracted. Several haunts hunkered down in the kitchen. None spoke to me, but they all stared at me with great intensity. All except for Bartholomew Foster, but the deep voids where his eyes had once been pointed at me, so I suspected he, too, was staring.

Midnight appeared next to me as Mom placed the waffles in front of me. On edge from hearing voices and all the staring ghosts, the clatter of the plate startled me a bit. I recoiled as the plate hit the table.

"They're just waffles, sweetie. They won't hurt you," Mom said and pulled out a chair.

"It's *not* the waffles, Mom!" I snapped, immediately regretting my harsh tone. "It's not you. It's everything. I'm sorry. It's just that there are..." I paused, looking around the room and counting ghosts, "seven human spirits and a ghost cat. In the kitchen right now. It's distracting."

Midnight mewed, annoyed that he had been included in the group of distracting haunts.

"Sorry, Midnight," I said in reply. "I like having you here." He meowed back an approving little mew. "As for the rest you. I like you. I want to help you. But can I please eat breakfast with my parents?"

With a few grunts, groans, grumbles, and one, "Well I never!" the ghosts dissipated, all save for Midnight who stood a bit taller knowing he was always welcome. Ghost or not, he was still a cat, and cats tend to think they rule the world, after all.

My parents' jaws dropped, unused to me being so open about my magical abilities. Though they now knew the truth about me, they hadn't wrapped their minds around it yet. We all needed time to adjust. If the pale looks on their faces were any indicator, it was going to take some time.

"Is it always like that? Seven ghosts at breakfast?" Dad asked, trying but failing to hide his shock.

"Not usually seven for one meal, but yeah. They are always here. There are thousands of ghosts in this town, and I am the only person who can talk to them, so they all come by a lot."

"And it's always been this way?" Mom asked.

I nodded.

"As long as I remember. I've been told that I interacted with them even as a baby. I don't remember a time when they were *not* there. Especially Midnight," I gestured to the kitty even though I knew my parents couldn't see him. "He's been here every single day. It might sound silly to you, but he is my best friend."

The cat meowed and rubbed himself against me, sending a familiar chill down my spine.

"Honey, I'm so sorry. I guess I thought you just had imaginary friends like other kids. It seemed a bit strange that it kept up as you got older." Mom's face looked pained, years of regret obvious in her watery eyes.

"Don't be sorry. Let's just try and learn together," I said, resting my hand on her shoulder.

Mom smiled at me although I could see she was fighting back tears. We'd both been through a lot the past few days. I reminded myself that she had to make sense of her own childhood and repressed magical ability.

"There's something else," I said softly, tears filling my eyes as the previous day's conversation with Thomas and Polly came back to me.

"What's wrong?" Mom's voice was filled with concern.

"The ghosts. They're running out of time."

"How?" Dad asked.

"Some of them are fading away. Disappearing for long periods. They're worried that if the spell isn't broken quickly, they will cease to exist altogether." My face was soaked with the tears I couldn't fight back.

Mom's hand rose to her mouth.

Dad, obviously wanting to ease the tension in the room, suggested that we get ready to head to the cabin.

"Anything to get this moving faster," I agreed.

I went upstairs, shooed some spirits out of the shower, and turned the water on as hot as I could get it. I took out my phone and put on my favorite band, turning the volume up loud enough so I could hear it over the shower. Steamy water beat down on my skin. I closed my eyes and enjoyed a rare moment of peace.

It truly was a moment because the second I stepped out of the steamy shower, Polly appeared.

"Polly, please!" I gasped as I grabbed a towel off the rack on the wall.

"Sorry, sorry. I just wanted to wish you luck today. I hope you find something at Lavina's cabin."

"I'll try my best. Pol, you know I love you like my dead sister, but will you please leave so I can get dressed alone?"

Polly disappeared with a poof. I got dressed, throwing on a gray t-shirt and matching jeans and headed downstairs. Dad sat on the sofa, waiting for me.

"Let's go, kiddo," he said cheerfully.

"Okay," I replied, less cheerful. I couldn't help but feel that our plan was hopeless. Was I supposed to paw through the old witch's stuff until I found something that would tell me what happened? It didn't seem likely, but I didn't know what else to do, so I walked over to the cabin with my dad.

Everyone walked in Tansy. It's not that cars were banned. It's just the town was so tiny that taking a car was impractical. You could walk from the north end to the south end of town in precisely fourteen minutes. None of the six businesses even had a parking lot. What was the point?

As Dad and I walked through town, Midnight followed behind us. Dad tried to make conversation with me, but I was distracted. My thoughts darted around, hopping from topic to topic in a game of mental pinball. *Is it even worth going back to the cabin? How is Dad feeling? Will the kids at school realize I'm even weirder now? How will I ever solve this mystery?* Soon we'd reached the right spot at the edge of town. We hopped the wall and walked into the woods. I pointed out the remnants of the old path, and we followed it in silence until the cabin came into view.

"Wow! Check this place out! It's like something out of a movie!" Dad said.

"It's pretty amazing, isn't it?" I agreed.

This time, I came prepared for the dark, dusty cabin and brought along a few flashlights. We got to work, putting anything that looked like it could possibly be useful into my backpack. Soon it overflowed with books, vials, faded papers, a locket, and anything else we thought a witch might have used to practice magic. I even grabbed an old dress, in case having Lavina's clothes could somehow help. After a few hours, we'd emptied the cabin of almost anything that wasn't furniture or kitchenware. We decided to call it a day and head home.

Just as we were about to leave, I heard the voice from my room again.

"Look under the mattress," the voice called.

Either I'm going crazy, or someone is trying to help me, I thought.

"One sec, Dad. I need to check something," I told him as I walked across the room and groped around under the musty mattress. Dad opened his mouth like he wanted to question me, but he zipped his lips and watched. I lifted each corner of the mattress, not sure what I hoped to find. After a minute of this, I started to think that maybe the voice was leading me astray because I hadn't found anything other than three-hundred-year-old dust. *Eeew.*

That's what I get for listening to bodiless voices, I thought, but my hand hit something smooth. I grabbed it and pulled it out. It was a small, leather-bound book.

"What's that?" Dad called from across the room.

"I'm not sure," I said as I sat down on the bed to inspect it further.

The old book opened stiffly to reveal pages yellowed by age and covered in handwritten text. After reading a few lines, I realized what I'd found.

"It's a journal. Lavina's journal!" A shiver shot down my spine. A peek inside of the mind of the witch who cursed the town seemed like a clue worth finding.

A MOUNTAIN OF EVIDENCE

Once Dad and I returned home, we went directly up to my bedroom with all of the items we'd found in the cramped cabin. We dumped the overflowing contents of my backpack onto my bed. The sight was overwhelming. Where could I even start?

"I've got to go to the bank for a bit, buddy," Dad said. I nodded and thanked him for his help.

I took a few steps back and surveyed the stash. Unsure of what to do, I decided to sort the items into categories. First, I made a giant jumble of books. I counted—there were thirteen. With the three I'd retrieved on my first trip to the cabin, that made sixteen. That was much more work to read than the summer reading list my teacher had assigned! The next category was vials for potion making. There were forty-three. Age rendered many of the labels illegible, but I wondered if I might be able to find out what was in them somehow.

"Maybe I should call Grandma," I said aloud to no one in particular.

"Meow," replied Midnight, startling me with his presence.

"You think I should call?" I asked again, now that I knew he was there.

"Mew," he replied, looking deep into my eyes. Once again, it felt as if the feline knew more than I did.

"Okay, okay. I'll call."

Midnight purred as I dialed the phone. Grandma Gertrude picked up on the first ring.

"I thought you'd be calling," she said. "I just had a feeling."

"Does that happen often?" I asked. "Do you know a lot of things before they happen?" *Can Grandma read my mind?* The thought sent butterflies to my stomach.

"I wouldn't say I *know*. But I do get a lot of feelings—vibrations of future truths, especially from those whom I am most connected. So. You need help with mountains of magical research."

"Um. Yes. I do." Astounded that my grandma could sense so much, I added, "There's so much and I don't have a clue where to start."

"Okay. I can't come today, but I promise I will be there tomorrow right after sunrise."

"You don't have to come that early, Grandma. I don't wake up that early."

"Oh, right. You're almost thirteen now. Thirteen-year-olds don't get up at sunrise in the summertime, do they? Okay. How about I get there at nine a.m?"

"That sounds significantly superior to sunrise."

"Good. I'll see you then, sweetheart."

"Grandma?" I had to ask her about the ghosts fading before she got off the phone. With so much to explain before, I hadn't told her.

"Yes?"

"There's something else. The ghosts told me something. We're running out of time to break the curse."

"Running out of time?"

"The ghosts are disappearing."

I explained the situation. Grandma agreed that we needed to finish our work as soon as possible. She said she'd do some reading of her own before she came over in the morning in case she could find anything out about how long ghosts can stay on earth in the afterlife.

After thanking Grandma, I hung up the phone and turned back to the pile on my bed. I noticed Lavina's journal sitting on top of the pile. I opened it to the first page and read the words the witch wrote three hundred years ago.

I've built a cabin on the outskirts of the most adorable village. It's called Tansy. So far, the people are suspicious of me. I hope I can convince them not to fear me. I am a bit lonely out here in the forest.

She didn't seem scary. I flipped the pages forward and kept reading.

I have been trying so hard to win over the people of Tansy. On the other side of town, there is a field that grows the most beautiful petunias. I thought that I would share the beauty I see when wandering in the wilderness with the townspeople. I picked dozens and dozens of flowers. It took hours. I carried them across town while everyone was asleep and put them all in front of the post office. Shortly after sunrise, Postmaster Gleason arrived for a day of work and saw me as I placed the last of the flowers around the window. He yelled at me and told me to leave. I tried to explain that I just wanted to share the beautiful flowers with the town. He didn't care. He said the flowers were likely cursed. I ran away, crying.

I wondered if Postmaster Gleason was the cranky ghost who refused to speak to me and haunted the post office. The others called him Mr. Gleason. I'd always assumed he was a relative of Tara's. I made a mental note to ask Thomas about him. The more I read, the less threatening the witch in the woods seemed. I flipped through the journal's worn pages and found another entry.

I baked biscuits and took them to the bank today. I hoped that sharing a treat with the townspeople would help them to understand that they need not fear me. I walked in with a basket overflowing with buttery biscuits and smiled at the banker, Mr. Penderbrook. I explained that I wanted to leave the biscuits somewhere all could enjoy them. He knocked the basket onto the floor and accused me of trying to poison the town. He said that the citizens of Tansy were becoming weary of me and had banded together to "take care of the problem." I know not what he means by this, but I am afraid.

He went on to say that a boy from the village sneaked into my cabin last year. He saw my books on witchcraft and reported back to his family that I was a witch. A week later, the poor child died in a farming accident. The people of the town think I cursed him for breaking into my home. I'd never kill anyone, let alone a child! But they've made up their minds, and their anger is tangible.

My heart sank. Poor Lavina. She tried so hard to be nice to the town. Empathy for the lonely witch rose up within me. I flipped to the back of the book.

They've done it. After months of talking about it, the townspeople have officially banished me from ever entering Tansy again. All I wanted was their friendship. I secretly helped their crops grow with white magic. When their children were sick, I put healing spells over their homes while they slept. They never knew what I did for them, and now they never will. I'm devastated. Beyond that, my bones are filled with rage. I wish to find a way to get back at them for being so unkind and ungrateful. I know not how to work dark magic, yet I find myself wishing I did.

I found myself sympathizing with Lavina more than the townspeople. She shouldn't have cursed the town, but she seemed lonely and sorrowful, not angry and evil. I couldn't wait to discuss all of this with Grandma the next day.

I looked back at the pile on my bed. Though I'd made some headway in sorting the hodgepodge of magical miscellany, the thought of continuing to organize it boggled my mind. I sat down and halfheartedly began picking out all of the personal items that once belonged to Lavina: the silver locket, a comb, the dress, a pair of gold glasses with round frames, and a black hat. I set them aside in a small stack next to my dresser.

The pile on the bed seemed to taunt me. *You don't even know what you're looking for,* the whispers in the back of my mind told me. *You'll never help the ghosts.*

"Ugh!" I called out. "I can't take another second of this. I need a break!"

I raced out of the room, slamming the door behind me. I plowed down the stairs in such a rush that I tripped and rolled the rest of the way to the bottom. A yelp escaped my lips, and tears welled up in my eyes. I sat up, head spinning, and realized that I was truly injured. My left leg throbbed with pain. As I removed my sneaker and pulled up my pant leg to inspect my injury better, I watched in amazement as my leg swelled before my eyes. By the time I had my sock off, it was more than twice its typical size and extremely red.

"Oh, no!" I cried out. "No, no, no! I don't have time for this!" I sobbed, heaving uncontrollably. With everything going on, hurting my leg seemed like one thing too many, and I broke down, overcome with pain and frustration.

"No! No! No!" Petey the parrot called from his cage. I despised that bird.

Sitting on the cold wood floor, I strained my neck to see out the bay window into the driveway. My parents' cars weren't there. Panic started to set in. How was I supposed to handle this on my own?

If I can get to my phone, I can get Mom here to help, I thought, looking across the room to the spot I'd left my cell phone after my conversation with Grandma. It sat on a table about twenty feet away.

I tried to pull myself up on the banister. It was then that I noticed the bruises that were beginning to form all over my arms. It took three tries, but finally, I managed to stand up on one foot. Sweat dripped from my forehead, and tears and snot covered my face. I was glad Tara wasn't around to see me like this. If she were, she'd have a field day with it. I took a deep breath. *You can do this,* I thought. I hopped forward once, twice, three times. I stopped, resting my arm on an end table before hopping again. I took three more hops and was about halfway to my phone, exhausted from my injury and stress. I hopped again, and my foot caught the red woolen rug on the floor. I fell, hitting the hardwood with a thud that reverberated throughout the empty house.

This time, only my ego was injured. Midnight appeared, meowing at me encouragingly as I sat up. I decided to scoot the rest of the way to the phone on my bottom. I felt ridiculous, but it got the job done, and I soon made it to my phone. I reached up to the tabletop and pulled it down.

I dialed my mom, who promised to rush home from work. I rested as I waited.

"Well, I really screwed that one up, didn't I, Kitty-Cat?" I said to Midnight, who purred back at me. He dissipated and came back a few moments later with Polly.

"Aww, did you get me a friend to wait with? Thanks, Midnight," I praised my ghoulish kitty.

"Are you alright, Grace?" Polly asked.

"It hurts. A lot. My mom's coming, though."

Polly seemed relieved. I waited with my friend and my kitty for the twenty-five minutes it took Mom to get to the house. My heart rate slowed as their presence comforted me. There's nothing quite like a good friend when you're feeling down, even if they're dead.

The sound of a car door slamming and footsteps flying up the front porch alerted us to Mom's arrival. Midnight and Polly disappeared as the door burst open. Mom rushed to me, inspected my leg, and insisted that we drive right back to the hospital.

At the hospital, the doctor took one look at my leg and sent me off for x-rays. As soon as he saw the films, he diagnosed me with a broken fibula. Since the bone needed to set, he put me under anesthesia, and I fell asleep, my dreams a mirror of my anxiety and frustration. When I woke, a green cast adorned my leg, and Dad and my grandparents had joined Mom at my bedside.

"When can I go home?" I asked as soon as I could form the words from my sleepy state.

"Soon," Mom told me. "We were just waiting for you to wake. I'll get the doctor."

As soon as the doctor signed a few forms, we headed to the parking lot of the hospital. Dad pushed me to the car in a wheelchair. Frustrated with myself for being so careless, I felt heat rising in my cheeks. My left leg throbbed with pain, and all the medicine I'd been given made me groggy. Tears welled in my eyes but I did my best to keep them at bay. Grandma leaned over, hugged me, and reminded me that she'd be by in the morning. The arduous task that lay ahead of me all came rushing back to me, and then the tears did come.

How am I going to help the ghosts now? I thought, sniffling for much of the car ride back to Tansy.

When I got home, I wanted to go directly to bed. I couldn't get to my bed, however, and I had to sleep on the couch. I hated sleeping on the sofa. I liked the security and privacy of my bedroom. It didn't matter, in the end, because the medication made me so exhausted that I slept anyway. It seemed like moments before morning came with sunbeams shining down on my face.

It was a new day, and I hoped it would be a better one.

Before I could open my eyes, it happened again. I heard a whisper that seemed far, far away.

"The mirror. Don't forget the mirror."

I sat up with a start. Not a soul, living or dead, was in the room with me.

VISITING GRANDMA GERTRUDE

Grandma Gertrude was true to her promise and arrived precisely at nine a.m. She brought with her an armful of baked goods: muffins, croissants, bagels, and coffee cake.

"I wasn't sure what you'd want to eat, so I bought out the bakery," Grandma explained when she saw my wide eyes.

We sat on the sofa and ate. I chose a blueberry bagel and smeared some jam on it with a plastic knife Grandma produced from the bakery bag. We ate in silence for a few moments before Grandma spoke.

"I'm sorry about your setback, sweetie. I know this has to be incredibly frustrating for you."

I nodded, not even sure if I could talk about it without getting upset again.

"I'm here now. I'll help however I can."

Grandma wrapped her wrinkled arms around me. I leaned into her, taking in her familiar lavender scent. Sometimes, you just need your grandma. Everything seemed better because Grandma Gertrude was by my side.

Grandma began to tell tales of her time living in this house, practicing magic with a small group of sorceresses. Her gray eyes sparkled as she spoke of spectacular spells and powerful potions. Fascinated to know her in this way, I listened intently.

"I'll never forget the time that Beatrice Bello accidentally turned

Tina Goodacher into a turtle! Oh, how we laughed. Well, all of us except for Tina. Turtles can't laugh." Grandma chuckled, her face twisting into a wrinkled grin. "Tina was returned to her human form soon enough, but it made for quite an afternoon."

"Bello? As in Bain Bello?" I asked, surprised to hear my classmate's name. Or was he my friend? He called me his friend. I blushed thinking about Bain.

"Beatrice had a boy called Alec, who I believe did have a son called Bain."

"So, there are still other magical families living in Tansy?" I asked, my mind whirling. *Was Bain a witch? What do you call a boy witch?*

"I know some of the same families still live here. I don't know, however, if any of them still practice magic. I didn't keep in touch."

I felt a bit let down for a moment, afraid that there was no one left to share this part of me with, but quickly recovered my excitement. Bain *might* be magical. He might be my friend, my living friend, and he might be someone I could talk to about all of this. And it didn't hurt that he was kind of cute. My heart fluttered.

After breakfast, I asked Grandma if she would go upstairs to my bedroom and grab the items that I'd retrieved from Lavina's cabin. She lugged them back downstairs and set the collection on the coffee table in front of us.

We stared at the items. The pile of precious and peculiar things seemed to glow with a faint light of possibility. Grandma fingered the silver locket, inspecting it closely. I showed her Lavina's journal, and she paged through it for quite some time. I remembered momentarily that the mirror was still out in the shed and was about to tell Grandma when she held up the mildewy map and let out a gasp.

"This is amazing!" The corners of Grandma's lined mouth turned up into a smile.

"Isn't it? Look, the house is marked on the map!" I pointed it out, and the mirror flew out of my mind.

We spent the rest of the morning looking over Lavina's map and talking about the tantalizing possibilities the town of Tansy had to offer. Grandma couldn't wait to inspect the field where the "sacred berry" grew. She told me that it was useful in potion-making and that fairies eat it almost exclusively. Fairies! I couldn't wait until my leg healed so that I could explore Tansy, map in hand.

I couldn't remember having so much fun with my grandma. I'd always loved Grandma Gertrude, but now I felt closer to her than ever before. It was as if the sisterhood of sorcery knit our souls together.

The day flew by, and, after what seemed like only minutes, it was late afternoon, and Grandma needed to leave. As she rose to go, her face dropped. "I didn't want to spoil our day together, but I can't put off telling you any longer. I found a book about spirits, Grace. It belonged to my mother. It said that human spirits who don't pass into the Light will eventually die a spiritual death. The spiritual lifespan tends to be about three hundred years after death, but it can range between 250 and 350 years. You are right when you say your friends have limited time."

My jaw dropped. I hoped there was another explanation, but many of the ghosts in town would be gone forever if I didn't act fast. She pulled me into a hug. "I am so sorry, sweetheart. I promise you that I will try to help in any way I can."

She brushed her hand against my cheek, stroking my face as she did when I was a toddler. The pain in my chest was too strong for me to find words. I nodded slightly as Grandma bid me goodbye and left.

Only a short pang of discouragement that we hadn't solved the mystery flashed through me as the door closed behind Grandma. Bonding and learning about magic were important, too.

As her car pulled out of the driveway, I heard the voice again.

"The mirror! Don't forget the mirror!"

I tried to sit up straight as I turned my head in every direction, trying to find the source of the voice. I didn't see a soul, living or dead. The speaker wanted their identity to remain a mystery, or so it seemed.

"Who are you? Why don't you show yourself?" I called out in frustration, but the empty room gave no reply.

The weight and bulk of my casted leg became increasingly evident when I attempted to rise so I could get my crutches and head out to the shed. Pain shot down my leg, knocking me back onto the sofa.

There's no way I'm making it out to the shed on my own, I thought. *I wish there were someone around to help.*

In a moment filled with a combination of bravery and desperation, I snatched my phone off the cluttered glass coffee table. Ringing filled my ear before I even realized what I'd done.

WHAT DID I DO?

"Hello?"

"Um." I gasped. *What am I doing?* Sweat slid off my skin as I staggered for breath. Why had I called Bain? My cheeks flushed with embarrassment.

"Is someone there? Grace?"

"Um, yes. Sorry. It's Grace." *Caller I.D. Of course he knows who's calling!*

"Hi, Grace. You okay? You sound weird."

What I wanted to say, but couldn't, was that I suspected that maybe, just maybe, he had magic powers and that's why I called. That would be too much, even for the strange girl in gray who saw ghosts.

Instead, I said, "I broke my leg."

"Oh no! I'm sorry!" Bain's voice actually sounded concerned.

"I. Um. I'm home alone for the next few hours, and I'm having a really hard time getting around and stuff. I was wondering if you wouldn't mind coming over? Helping me out with a few things? I'm sorry for pestering you. I understand if you have something else to do, I mean, um," I rambled. My face burned.

"Grace, it's fine. I'd be happy to come over," Bain interrupted.

"You would? Okay. Wow. Thanks!"

"It's not a problem. I'm sorry you're hurt. I'll be by soon, okay?"

"Okay. See you soon."

The call disconnected, and I stared at the phone. I'd called because I wanted assistance looking through Lavina's things; however, I couldn't ask him for help unless I knew I could trust him with all things magical. I couldn't know that unless I asked. But how do you just come out and ask someone something like that and not sound insane?

Bain only lived a short walk from my house. To be fair, Tansy was so tiny that everyone in town only lived a short walk from my house. I didn't have long to try to hide Lavina's things, which were still spread out on the coffee table. My limited mobility didn't make this any easier, and in the end, I awkwardly tossed a hoodie over the top of the items right as the doorbell rang.

My leg pulsed with pain, so instead of trying to hop to the door, I called out, "Come in!" Tansy wasn't the kind of town where people locked their homes in the middle of the day.

The door opened, casting a light into the living room from the bright summer day outside. Bain walked through the doorway and smiled at me, the sun catching in his brown eyes, making the specks of green sparkle more than usual. He brushed his black hair away from his face, closed the door, walked over to the sofa, and sat down next to me. My heart fluttered as his knee bumped my own.

"Look at that," he said, pointing to my cast. "What a bummer. How'd you do it?"

"I fell down the stairs," I admitted, feeling dumb.

"Ouch! Well, I'm glad you called."

"You are?" I felt my cheeks flush. Why did that always happen around Bain?

"Yeah. I mean, you shouldn't be stuck here without help all day."

"Oh," I said, feeling a bit let down. Maybe he didn't like me. Maybe he just came because he's a nice person. "My grandma was here for a while, but she had to go."

"Still, I'm certain it's not how you wanted to spend your summer."

"No. It's not," I said quietly. Then my eyes widened. Thomas

Meyer appeared, floating around Bain's face. This wasn't the time for invisible visitors!

"Yeah, you're supposed to be helping us!" Thomas insisted.

Thomas had a way of putting himself in the middle of just about any situation. Sometimes it was helpful, like with the bullies at school. Right now, however, he was making me grouchy. I couldn't say anything to him. Or even look at him for more than a moment, because Bain might think it strange if I shot searing stares at empty space.

I attempted to adjust my focus to Bain. Smiling shyly at my classmate, I searched for the words that could start a conversation about magic.

"So, my grandma was telling a story about old friends of hers, and I think one of those friends might have been a relative of yours."

"Well, that wouldn't be surprising. She grew up here in Tansy, right?"

"Yes. So, is Beatrice Bello your relative?"

"That would be my father's mother." Bain smiled.

"Ah! Well, I guess our grandmothers were friends!" I said.

Thomas whooshed by my head and laughed. I shot him a look and tried to think of what I should say next. I may have broken the ice about Bain's grandma, but I didn't know how to transition from an old friendship to gatherings of sorcery. It turned out I didn't have to figure out what to say next because Bain did it for me.

"That was back when the gatherings met here, right?"

"The...gatherings?" I sputtered, caught off guard.

"Yeah, the coven, the meetings of our people."

"Our...people?" I twisted a curl around my finger.

"Am I telling you something you don't know about? I, um, maybe —maybe you should talk to your grandma about it," Bain bumbled.

"No, I know. I just found out, but I know. I wasn't sure if *you* knew." I spoke quickly, my voice mimicking my accelerated heartbeat.

"Wait, you *just* found out?"

"Yeah. A few days ago."

Bain knew this huge thing about me all along, and I'd been clueless. I attempted to push away the growing sense of foolishness that swam up my gut.

"That kind of makes sense," he answered after a few moments. "That you didn't know. You're always disappearing in a crowd, but it sometimes seems unplanned."

"It's sort of always unplanned," I admitted awkwardly. "No one told me. I just thought I was weird. I didn't know I was..."

"Magic?" Bain suggested, smiling.

"Well, yeah. I had no clue." I couldn't help smiling back.

"Wow, I can't even imagine not knowing. I've known my whole life. Both of my parents and my sister practice magic, as well. It's just a way of life in our house."

"My grandma hid it from my mom, so my mom never knew, so she never told me."

"Wow." Bain shook his head in bewilderment.

"Yeah. It's been a lot of both of us to take in."

"I bet. So, um, what can you do?"

"What can I *do*?"

"Yeah, like, are you a fireshifter or a naturemorph or what? I mean, obviously, you've got the vanishing thing down, but someone with your lineage would probably have several skill sets."

"Well, I moved a spoon with my mind the other day."

"Ah, mattermorphing. Cool."

"Yeah, I'm still working on that. And there's this other thing. Probably my main skill." I paused a moment, preparing myself for how he might react. "I see the dead. And talk to them. There's a ghost floating by your head. And a few in the kitchen."

Bain's brown eyes bulged, and his jaw dropped. "You're a spirittalker? That's super rare. I've never met one before. I mean, I've met you lots of times, but I didn't know." He turned around, his eyes darting around the room as he attempted unsuccessfully to see the spirits.

"That's what my grandma said. It's just normal to me. There are always ghosts around. What about you? What do you do?"

Bain lifted his left hand, and little lavender flames danced in his palm.

"Cool!"

He smiled, closed his palm, then opened it again, and water shot out of his hand and across the room. Moments before it splashed all over the wall, he closed his palm and it turned to ice. As the frozen stream headed for the floor, Bain shifted his head slightly and it disappeared.

"Wow! That's super impressive!"

Bain shrugged. His full lips turned upward ever so slightly, so I could tell that he appreciated my praise.

"I'm an embermage. Though it sounds like embers only manipulate flames, many of us control all the elements—wind, water, earth, and fire."

"I don't know a lot about this. My grandma hasn't really given me a lot of information, and my mom might be even more clueless than I am. But I thought you were a witch? Er, a boy witch? Are male witches something different?"

"Um. We prefer the term mage." Bain cringed as he spoke.

"Is witch a bad term?" I realized that my grandma had never used the word "witch."

"Well. A lot of negative connotations are associated with the term witch. Not just because it sounds like it should be a lady."

I nodded, thinking of my dream.

"And even when you look past that—it's not what our people are. Witches practice a set of beliefs. We don't. We come from all faiths, all walks of life, but what binds us goes deeper than even that. It's our blood. We all come from magical families. Our power, our wizardry, if you will, is in us from our first breath. There have been those over the years who also practiced witchcraft, of course, but as people, we are not witches. We are the Mages of Nixie."

"Mages of Nixie," I repeated. "So, do we all live near Lake Nixie? Are there other groups in different towns or what?"

"There are clusters of magical peoples all over the world. But Lake Nixie is full of magic. Its power flows through our veins."

"So, wait, the whole town is magic?" I asked, confused. When I first thought Bain could be like me, it made sense. We were the oddballs, the other-worldly, the unlikable kids at school. But if the whole school was filled with mages, well, it just meant I was still weird, even among the strange.

"Oh, no. Just those of us who have ancestors who were here for the founding of Tansy. There are only seven families left. Eight if we count yours, but we haven't since your grandma turned her back on it all. From what I understand, they used to meet here, at this house, before we were born, but when your grandma left, we moved the gatherings to the field on the edge of town. We still meet on Mondays in the moonlight. A few kids from school are mages. No one else in our class, but there are a few kindergarteners this year, and a few kids in the upper classes. Do you know Sophia? She's a few grades ahead of us."

I nodded. I had a hard time taking it all in. The room seemed to sway, the sunlight shifting into swirls of smoke around me. Relieved to already be seated, I leaned back on the sofa and closed my eyes.

"Are you okay?"

"I'm overwhelmed. This has been quite the week."

Bain put his hand gently on my shoulder. Warmth seemed to radiate from his hand, and my heart, my erratically beating heart, slowed to its normal pace.

"It's a calming charm," Bain told me. "My mom is a healer. She tries to teach me her skills. I'm no good at healing bones." He looked at my leg sympathetically. "But I'm pretty good at extinguishing anxiety."

We sat like that for several minutes. It was nice to be close to a living person. After I was calm, I remembered the mirror, the ghosts, and my quest. The charm worked so well that none of it seemed insane any longer.

"There is one thing I know that I am pretty sure you don't," I began, studying Bain's face for clues as to how this made him feel. His eyebrows raised, but he said nothing. "This town is cursed. The living are fine. But the dead are stuck. Every single soul who has ever lived in or passed through Tansy for over three hundred years is trapped in this town and can't move on into the Light. There are thousands upon thousands of ghosts here. The spirits stay not because they want to, but because a witch named Lavina cursed them. Well, maybe she wasn't a witch?"

It took Bain a second to respond. "No, she was a witch. I know who you're talking about. She's legendary. She's the reason why we're so secretive with our magic. But what you're saying about the ghosts—you say there are thousands? That's crazy! How many are in other towns?"

I shrugged. "A handful? I don't spend tons of time in other towns, but usually, people don't stick around Earth long after they've died. Here, the dead are unable to leave."

"Wow," Bain said. The look on his face seemed to indicate that he was pondering the massive number of spirits the village possessed.

"Yeah. And they asked me to break the curse."

"No wonder you're freaking out."

"And worse yet, their time is running out. Apparently, spirits can only stay on Earth for a limited time before their soul's lifespan ends. If they don't go into the Light soon, a lot of them will cease to exist."

"Whoa," Bain said, his eyebrows raised.

I turned my head to the coffee table and pulled my hoodie off the heap of items from Lavina's house.

"I got all of this from Lavina's cabin just outside of town, but there's one more thing out in the shed. And, um. A voice has been asking to look at it."

"A voice? Like a ghost?" Bain asked.

"Well, I can see the ghosts. At least, I usually can. This is a bodiless voice. It calls to me when no one else, living or dead, is around."

Now I sound totally insane. I hope Bain doesn't think I am, I thought.

"Whoa," he said again, running his hand through his long hair.

"But I can't get out to the shed right now," I said, looking down and biting my lip.

"Ah. *That's* why you called."

"Yes," I said, shrugging.

"Well. I guess I better get out to that shed then," he said with a smile.

THE MIRROR

Several minutes later, Bain set the silver mirror on the sofa. I had forgotten how intoxicating its beauty was. I picked it up and peered into its foggy glass, staring into its silvery surface, searching for what to do next.

I set it down and shrugged. "I don't know what we're supposed to do with it, but the voice kept telling me to get it."

Bain picked it up again, inspecting every inch of it intently. He rubbed some dust off the back, squinted, then rubbed it again.

"Odd as it may be, an inscription is before me." There he went, speaking in riddles again, like he always did at school.

I reached for the mirror, and he placed it in my hands. I wiped away a bit more dust and read:

What makes a day?
What might one's actions say?
If others could watch for twenty-four hours
What would they learn of your powers?
Speak to the mirror and you shall see
A single day for a witch like me.

"So, we're supposed to talk to the mirror and it will show us a day in her life?" I asked, barely able to suppress my skepticism.

"So it seems," Bain said, his voice full of disbelief.

"Okay," I said, feeling exceedingly foolish. "Mirror, show us what you can."

The foggy glass came to life. Swirling silvery clouds swayed and swooshed for several seconds on its surface. The fog cleared, and the mirror's glass showed the inside of Lavina's cabin as it was over three hundred years before.

"Wow," Bain whispered, his tone almost reverent.

"Wow," I agreed.

We watched as Lavina became visible on the glass. She paced back and forth across the tiny cabin. Her long white hair flowed in wispy waves over her ivory dress. Her wrinkled hand found its way to the ends of her hair, tugging from time to time as she paced. A black cat occasionally rubbed up against her ankles, but she ignored it.

"I am not but kind to these people and they banish me! *Banish!*" Her voice was filled with hurt and contempt.

She paced some more and then headed to the bookshelf and pulled down a book of spells. The mirror seemed to speed up the old witch's pace as she flipped through the book, muttering to herself. After several minutes of this, it slowed to a normal pace.

Lavina pointed her bony finger at a page of the book and cackled, throwing her head back as she laughed heartily. "If they don't want me here, they'll never leave! I'll trap them in this tiny town for the rest of their lives!"

The mirror fast-forwarded Lavina's motions as she wandered through the cabin, gathering a few items and tossing them into a satchel. She paced the length of the room several more times, tears falling from her tormented turquoise eyes at each turn.

The mirror slowed to show Lavina standing in the doorway. She looked at the black cat at her feet. "It's decided," she said to the cat. "I shall curse this vile village and leave forever. The *Curse of Trapped Souls* will suit them just right."

"Write that down!" I told Bain, speaking for the first time in several minutes. I gestured toward a notepad on Dad's desk at the far end of the room. Bain sprinted to the desk, grabbed a pen, and scribbled down the name of the curse.

The mirror faded for a moment, then showed Lavina standing on the edge of town, near the west entrance of the stone wall. She raised her hands high above her head, tears still streaming down her wrinkled cheeks. Bain and I watched in silence as Lavina picked up some dirt from the ground, sprinkled it over the wall, and began to speak.

> *"The souls who pass here shall not leave*
> *and forever stay*
> *trapped inside to forever grieve*
> *this very day."*

Lavina reached into her white cloak and revealed a vial from which she pulled out what appeared to be a strand of golden hair. She placed it along the gate to the village and sobbed.

Just then, a young man stepped into the mirror's view. It was Thomas Meyer! He walked up to the open gate and right through it, stopping to look at Lavina momentarily.

"I thought they banished her," he said to himself, shaking his head as he walked down the path that led out of town.

Lavina's lips parted in surprise. "I've failed," she cried. "He left the village with ease! I never should have tried dark magic. I promised I'd only practice the Craft for good, and this is exactly what I deserve. Failure."

She walked down the path, head hanging in shame. The mirror swirled with smoke again for a few moments, and turned back to foggy glass.

I looked up at Bain and noticed several spirits gathering behind us, watching the mirror as well.

"It looks like we know what happened," I said, speaking to everyone in the room, living and dead alike.

"Yeah," said Bain, "but what do we do now?"

"I don't know," I sighed. "I really don't know."

THE CURSE OF TRAPPED SOULS

My first thought was that I needed Grandma Gertrude. Surely, Grandma had to know what to do. She had a lifetime of experience with magic.

"I'm calling my grandma," I told Bain and the sixteen spirits who now filled the room. Bain nodded. Several ghosts started whispering their thoughts on the situation. Bartholomew Foster bellowed, "I always knew it was that witch!" and shook his head back and forth, his face filled with an eyeless rage.

"Ssshh! Bartholomew! I am trying to make a phone call!" I scolded.

Bain opened his mouth to question me, but thought better of it, closed his mouth, and looked around the room for traces of my unseen friend. Still unable to see the ghosts, he shrugged, shook his head, and waited for me to make the call.

"Hi, Grandma," I said when she picked up the phone. "We figured out what she did to curse the town. Have you ever heard of *The Curse of Trapped Souls*?"

"That's not my brand of magic, but I just got back from Grandpa's doctor appointment. I'll be right over to help you figure this out."

An hour later, Grandma was sitting on the sofa with Bain and me. I explained to her what happened, how the mirror played back the last day Lavina had spent near Tansy, how she cursed the town and not known she'd actually succeeded. Grandma's eyes widened as I spoke.

"A Looking-Back Glass," Grandma said, her voice filled with awe.

"Can you tell me about it?" I asked, excited to learn whatever I could about the magic of the mirror.

"I've never actually seen one, just read about them. May I see?" Her eager hands motioned toward the silver mirror.

"Of course," I replied as I handed over the ancient looking glass.

"Hello, Looking-Back Glass," Grandma spoke slowly and clearly.

The mirror's glass became misty again and Lavina's day repeated. Though we'd viewed the same sequence not long before, Bain and I watched eagerly, examining the mirror for any minuscule details we might have missed. Grandma remained silent as she scrutinized the silvery mirror's show.

When it ended, Grandma carefully set the mirror down. She took a deep breath as if trying to calm herself a bit before speaking.

"You made the same assumptions I would have based on the information presented by the mirror. Unfortunately, I am not familiar with dark magic. There is a very good chance that if the original spell is in one of the books you brought back from the cabin, a counter-spell could be listed there. I think your search begins with the stack of books on the table." She nodded toward the coffee table and rose to her feet. "I have to get back to Grandpa, but I will make some calls, see if anyone I know can help."

She gave me a quick hug, said goodbye, and strolled to the front door. She put her wrinkled hand on the brass knob, took in a deep breath, and said, "Your grandpa isn't doing well, sweetheart. I thought you should know. The cancer is back. The doctors say that he has a fifty percent chance of making it through the year."

It felt like I'd been punched in the stomach. I couldn't lose Grandpa Steve. He was strong like the Fantasma Mountains. He always stood in the corners of my world; I knew where I would find him every single day. Nearly frozen with grief, I managed to say, "I'll be praying for him."

Grandma stood still, her hand still on the knob. "Gracie, I'd move the moon for you, and I want to help, but I might not be as available as I would like through all of this. There are so many appointments to keep. You kids are going to have to try to do this on your own."

I had never seen Grandma look so pale or so serious. She turned back to the door and opened it, then walked out of the house. The sound of the door closing rang through the room. No one spoke. Silence overwhelmed us as the enormity of the situation washed over us in oceanic waves. Tears trickled down my face.

Unable to speak, or even make eye contact with Bain, I stared out the window into my front yard. Memories unfolded like a movie in my mind. Grandpa teaching me to ride a bike in the driveway. The day he tried, and failed, to convince me I might be a good softball player. Wrestling with him in the yard.

I didn't want to lose him.

And then it hit me. Grandpa had spent much of his life in Tansy. He was doomed to be cursed. We *all* were. Whatever came after this life, the Light, or Heaven—he deserved it. He didn't deserve to be stuck here in the afterlife, whenever his time came. Be it now or twenty years from now. Even if it would hurt to say goodbye.

"Bain," I said, my voice weak. "The curse. It's not just those who are already dead that it will affect. Think about it. My..." I took in a deep breath, forcing myself not to cry. "My grandpa could be dead within a year. One day, we'll all die. This isn't just their curse. It's all of our curse."

Bain nodded. "You're right. Are you okay?"

I sniffled. "Yes. Let's break this curse. Let's make it better for all of the ghosts, past, present, and future." I stared back out the window again. My memories were so clear I felt like I'd been transported in time.

Midnight jumped up on the table, looked at the stack of books, and mewed. I snapped out of it and sat up straight.

"Do you think we should get to work, Kitty-Cat?"

Bain raised his eyebrows, and he scanned the room. "Ghost cat?" he asked.

"Oh, right. Midnight is my cat. I don't remember a day when he wasn't here with me. But yes, he's a ghost."

"Cool. How many ghosts are here now?" Bain asked.

I took a moment to count; my eyes darted around the room, counting ghostly heads. "Thirteen, if you count Midnight."

"Wow. Is it always like that?" Bain whispered, mouth wide.

"Wow. Is it always like that?" Thomas Meyer mocked.

My head whipped around toward Thomas in anger. "Thomas, stop. Bain is helping you. You should be thankful." I turned back to my living friend and explained, "Yes, Bain, it's not uncommon for several spirits to surround me."

Bain shook his head back and forth slowly, perhaps trying to contemplate what life might be like for me.

"Gracie! Boys have cooties! Why are you playing with a boooy?" Jenni whined.

"Yeah, Gracie! I know this boy has cooties!" Thomas said, giving her a high-five, and shooting me a big-brotherly grin.

"He does not have cooties, Jenni."

"Should I even ask?" Bain said.

"Kindergarten ghost," I said with a shrug.

"Okay, then," Bain said, throwing his arms in the air. "No cooties here, young ghostie."

Midnight meowed loudly at me three times in a row. I laughed and picked up a book. "My cat wants us to begin."

Bain and I poured over the parchment pages of potion books. We muddled through manuals on magic. A towering tome on transfiguration took forever to sort through. Page after page, chapter after chapter, we searched for a single spell. These ancient texts were not alphabetized. There was no table of contents to tell us to turn to page 394. All we could do was read each page, one at a time, and hope to find the curse we sought.

After a few hours of feverish page-turning, the front door creaked open, startling us as Dad entered the house. My father, who wasn't used to seeing me sitting on the sofa with a boy, stood silent in the doorway, staring at us for a moment, mouth agape.

"Hi, Dad. Bain came by to help me sort through all of Lavina's stuff. I couldn't get around with my broken leg, so he's been super helpful."

"Of course. Um. Bain knows about *Lavina*?" Dad whispered Lavina's name, eyebrows raised.

"Yeah. He's a mage, too. Did you know that's what we're called? The Mages of Nixie."

Bain nodded, looking as pleasant as possible with my dad staring him down.

"Hmm. Well. That's...good. Is your mother home yet?" Dad seemed quite overwhelmed by not only the boy on the couch but also by the magical powers the females of his home possessed.

"Nope."

"Okay. Well, I'll make some dinner. Is Bain staying?"

Dad and I turned our heads to look at Bain. I could tell by the look on his face that Bain wanted to stay to continue helping me. He started to say yes, but he looked back at Dad, who stood nearby with his arms crossed, wearing a scowl on his face, trying his best to make Bain feel unwelcome.

"I should get home. Mind if I take a book with me, so I keep searching for the spell before I sleep?"

"Please do. I really appreciate your help." I handed him a book. Our fingers brushed for a moment, causing my heart to beat faster.

"I'll ask my parents if they have any ideas. They don't work in dark magic, but you never know."

"Thank you," I replied, looking into his eyes and grinning.

Bain stared back a moment, but my dad's presence snapped us both into reality. Bain cleared his throat, grabbed his phone off the table, and hurried across the room to leave.

"I'll bring it back tomorrow," he said, holding up the heavy book.

"And I will let you know what I find out. Bye," he called out as he rushed out the door.

"Oh good, he's coming back tomorrow," Dad muttered under his breath.

Thomas popped up next to my shoulder and laughed, "Daddy doesn't like Bainy-boy any more than I do!"

"What?" I asked, knowing full well what my father said, and ignoring Thomas all together.

"Nothing, sweetheart. What do you want for dinner?" He walked into the kitchen before I could respond.

I spent the rest of the night searching for the spell to no avail. I finally fell asleep on the sofa, surrounded by spirits, a book of hexes still open on my lap, dreaming of curses and spell books.

THIRTY SECONDS OF INTENSE PAIN

It started like any other morning, really. That is, any other morning for a twelve-year-old mage who possessed the ability to see the dead. I woke early, the pain in my leg preventing me from getting the rest I needed. It was before sunrise when I gave up on falling back to sleep. This gave me the gift of a ghost-free living room for a few hours. The ghosts, knowing I have a penchant for sleeping in, rarely arrived before sunrise.

I sat up on the sofa, still unable to walk with ease. I tried to tame my wild hair, tucking a few frizzy curls behind my ear, stretched, and grabbed my glasses off the end table. I sighed, the combination of a night full of dead ends searching for spells, little sleep, and a sore leg weighing on me. I needed a win, a tiny shred of hope. I looked around the room, which was still dark, save for a nightlight in the hallway. I noticed my mom's brown suede jacket hanging on the rack by the front door, illuminated by the nightlight.

I can move that, I thought. *If I try hard enough, I can move that jacket.*

I hadn't tried to do any magic since the other day at Grandma's. Everything had been too crazy to stop and try to figure out how to work my powers. At this moment, however, I had peace, which I hoped would be useful in learning magic.

I stared at the jacket, willing it to move. It remained still. I tried again, imagining the coat swishing back and forth on the hanger. Still, it stayed motionless. I tried a third and a fourth time to no avail. With each failure, I became more and more frustrated. By my fifth try, hot angry tears fell from my eyes.

"I. Can. Do. This," I said in a low voice as I stared intently at the jacket. A rumbling growl emerged from deep within me, and the coat moved.

To be honest, more than just the coat moved. The whole rack moved. In fact, I managed to knock the entire thing over with a thud. Within seconds, my parents burst into the living room, worried that perhaps there was an intruder. Dad wielded a baseball bat like a sword.

They stood side by side, mouths wide, staring at the coat rack, which was now in the center of the room. Mom turned her head to look at me, still sitting on the sofa with tear-stained cheeks. Dad walked over to me, still unsure of what happened, and put his arms around me.

"You okay, kiddo?" he asked, his tone gentle and even.

"Yeah," I sniffled. "I was trying to move the coat. I think I might have overdone it."

"But how did you—"

"With my mind, Dad. I can move things with my mind. I'm just not very good at it." I hung my head.

"I'd say you did a bang-up job." Dad poked my ribs and laughed at his own joke.

"Why don't I make us some breakfast, and we can sit and talk about it," Mom suggested. "I still can't move anything." A mournful tone I wasn't used to rang out in her voice.

I attempted to force my lips to curve into a smile and nodded at Mom. There was no way any of us would be getting back to sleep now. A few minutes later, my parents whipped up some pancakes and eggs, and my family sat on the sofa and scarfed them down.

Mom and I talked about telekinesis. Dad listened and tried to be encouraging. In truth, he looked as if he felt helpless, which, I assume, is a horrible way for a father to feel. I tried to explain how it worked to Mom. This was difficult because I didn't understand it myself.

"The first time, I thought that if Grandma could lift you, I could move the spoon. And it worked. This time, I got angry with myself. I think it's connected to our emotions, but I'm not sure how to properly control it," I explained.

Mom nodded, taking in what I said. She looked at her keys on the coffee table and stared intently at them. After a moment, the keys twitched—the movement was tiny, but real. We all cheered together. Dad hugged Mom, and a smile spread across his face.

Maybe he'll get used to having a magical family after all. A warm sensation filled my belly.

Soon, my parents needed to leave for work. I said goodbye and settled in with the books again. I was looking through the last volume when I heard a knock at the door. I knew it was Bain. I smoothed out my hair and sat up a bit straighter.

"Come in!"

He walked through the door carrying the book he'd taken with him the night before.

"Any luck?" I asked, nodding toward the tome.

"None," he sighed. "You?"

"Nope," I said grimly. I'm not sure what we do now."

"Well, first thing. I talked to my mom about all of this. I hope that's okay."

Happy to have more experienced mages to consult, I nodded. I hoped Bain had some new insight after talking to his mom.

"So, Mom wants to come over and fix your leg. We can get a lot more done if you're not injured."

A smile filled my face."Can she really fix it? That would be amazing!"

"She can. The other thing she reminded me of is that over in Omyra there's a library with a secret section. The librarian is a mage. Not a Mage of Nixie, she's from a different sect and moved to the area years ago. I know not which sect from whence she hails."

There he went again. Bain couldn't help but get all poetic from time to time. I stared at him, and he blushed when he realized how over the top he sounded. He cleared his throat and continued.

"So, if you go to this librarian and prove that you're a mage, she will show you to the back where she's stashed stacks upon stacks of sorcery books. Something might just help."

"That sounds perfect!"

"Let me text my mom. She said she'd come right over to fix your leg and drive us over there if you were up to it all."

Fifteen minutes later, Brenda Bello bounced through the front door. She looked half her age, had hair the color of sunbeams, and eyes that sparkled the deepest of blues. Bain later told me that a little-known perk of being a healer is that one can heal the signs of aging and stay forever young. I hadn't spent much time around Mrs. Bello and was surprised that her appearance was so unlike her son's. Bain must have got his dark features from his dad.

"I hear we have a leg that needs fixing," Mrs. Bello said, a bit too cheerfully for my taste. She was talking to a twelve-year-old about a broken leg, not trying to talk a kitten down from a tree.

"Yes. Thank you," I replied.

Mrs. Bello sauntered across the room and took a quick inventory of the injuries. Her eyes stopped on my bruised arms.

"Those bothering you at all?" she asked.

I looked down at my bruises and nodded. My arms didn't hurt nearly as bad as my legs, but the feeling that flowed through them was far from pleasant.

"I'll fix those, too, sweetie. You certainly did take a tumble, didn't you?"

"Yeah," I chucked, "But you should see the other guy." I grimaced at my own bad joke, but Bain didn't seem to mind. His lips formed a smile, then he chuckled.

"I'm sure those stairs won't mess with you again!" he said.

A grin covered Mrs. Bello's face as she watched us interact.

"I'm going to heal you now, Grace. I wish there were a way

around that part. Thirty seconds of intense pain will make you as good as new, though. Are you ready?" Mrs. Bello's words were gentle as she rested her hands on my broken leg.

Intense pain? Haven't I had enough of that? But I said, "Yes, Mrs. Bello. I'm ready." I tried not to look afraid.

Mrs. Bello waved her hands over my injuries. A soft glowing white light poured out of her fingers and enveloped every inch of me. For a moment, warmth and an overwhelming sense of peace flowed through my body, but within seconds that security shattered into shards of searing pain. A scream escaped my throat with such force that it ached. My entire body writhed back and forth. I fell to my knees. My back arched high, like a cat's, and I began to shake. Just when I was sure the pain would end me, it stopped. I gasped, and sweat poured down my pounding head.

"I'm so sorry, baby. There's no way to prepare one for the pain that comes in healing. The thing is, you can speed up the recovery, but even the strongest sorcerers can't heal a broken bone in a way that is painless. All we can do is put all of the pain you would have experienced throughout the course of your injury to a few quick seconds. You should be able to stand now."

Still breathless and foggy-brained from the healing, I stood up. Bain took my hand as I got to my feet. At first, I only put weight on my uninjured leg. It had become second nature to move in a way that protected my injury.

Mrs. Bello nodded at me, encouraging me to let my casted leg take some of my body's weight. I closed my eyes as I let my foot hit the ground. To my surprise, I experienced not one bit of pain. It felt completely normal. I took a few painless steps. I hopped up and down several times. No pain! I bounced from the left leg to the right over and over again. I knew I looked like a nitwit, but freedom from the pain filled me with delight.

"It doesn't hurt!" I squealed. I realized that not only was I still holding Bain's hand, but I'd squeezed it tightly. I let go, my face burning with an embarrassed blush. I worried he would start to think that bright red was my natural skin tone.

"Thank you," I said as I turned to Mrs. Bello to avoid looking at Bain.

"You're welcome, dear. Now. Let's get you out of that cumbersome cast. This will be pleasantly painless."

She waved her hands and the cast split in two, clattering on the ground with a satisfying sound. My eyes widened at the sight of it all. My world had changed so much over the past week.

As if she hadn't just put my bones back together, Mrs. Bello looked at me and said cheerfully, "I hear you two might need a ride to the library?"

THE LIBRARY

Twenty-seven minutes later, Mrs. Bello dropped us off in front of the library, promising to pick us up when we were ready. She drove off quickly, in a rush to make it to Bain's sister's soccer practice. The Omyra Library was an ominous, over-sized oddity. Not a single building in any town in the Fantasma Mountains was this large. Its architecture seemed to suit a cemetery better than a library. A black wrought-iron gate encircled the gigantic gray building. Gargoyles gripped onto the grungy columns above the grubby shrubs in the sad little garden. This was one building that was terribly out of place in the picturesque mountain range.

"Wow," I whispered as we walked down the winding stone path toward the west entry.

"Amazing architecture awaits, for sure; are we asking too much to achieve answers as well?" Bain pondered.

"I hope we find something," I replied. I never knew how to respond when Bain spoke this way. It didn't bother me like it did many of our classmates. In fact, I reveled in Bain's eccentricities. His quirks were endearing.

The entry door to the library stood close to twenty feet high. Every inch of it was covered in intricate ironwork. It looked like it belonged in a museum. As I turned the knob, a shock shot through my body like nothing I'd ever felt before. This magnificent place was teeming with more magic than anywhere else in these mountains. The feeling upon entry was tantalizing.

Bain's mom had visited this collection of books many times before and instructed him on where to go. I followed, grateful that my friend had a grasp on what to do. He walked purposefully toward the desk and asked for Dora.

A few minutes later, a dark-skinned woman with wild hair and tidy clothes came to the desk. Her eyes flickered with recognition upon seeing Bain and a smile spread across her round lips.

"Mr. Bello! You're here! And who have you brought with you?" Her voice was raspy, as if she'd used it to speak the sentences of seven lifetimes, which, coincidentally, I later learned she had.

"This is Grace Aaronson," he told her. "She's the granddaughter of—"

"Gertrude! Gertrude Ermaldi! My goodness. She's the spitting image! It's as if time turned back and young Gertrude came walking into the library!"

I smiled. People always told me I looked like my grandma, but it never got old. I'd always enjoyed the comparison, and now that I knew Grandma Gertrude better and we shared more than gray eyes and high cheekbones, pride filled my entire being.

"We need to see the secret section, Dora," Bain whispered. "We have to break a curse."

Dora nodded as if this were normal. I wondered if maybe she heard this kind of thing all the time. With so many magical people living nearby, curses might not be so uncommon after all.

"So, what are we working with?" Dora asked in a hushed tone as we headed down the hallway. "Kissing curse? *Curse of the Crow*? Some sort of homework hex? Youthful curses are such an important part of mage mastery, as annoying as they are. These little curses you kids put on one another teach you how to handle yourselves with heavier hexing." She raised her eyebrows, then smiled like this was all a game.

All of those curses sounded downright fun in comparison to

Lavina's. I liked the idea of middle-school mages playing harmless tricks on one another. But that's not what this was.

"Actually, it's the *Curse of Trapped Souls*," I replied, trying not to let it sound as serious as it was.

"Oh, my. No, no, no. This won't do. Who on earth could have cast such a curse? That's not our way. That's dark witchcraft. That's not what mages do." Dora shook her head back and forth, clearly displeased with this news.

"Well. It wasn't a mage. It was Lavina, the White Witch of the Wood. And it happened three hundred years ago."

Dora stopped and stared deep into my eyes, her face searching for a hint of a joke or maybe a youthful misunderstanding. I nodded at the librarian slowly.

"Tansy? It's Tansy that's been cursed? And you are sure it worked? That spirits are trapped there in the afterlife? I don't think we even have a spirittalker in this community to confirm..." Her shoulders tensed.

"We have one," Bain said, looking at me.

"You—You're a spirittalker?" Dora asked, shaking her head, mouth wide.

I nodded again. "Since the day I was born, I've been surrounded by spirits. There are thousands of them in Tansy. Thousands."

"Well. Then you've got work to do," Dora said. "This way." She motioned to her left, and we followed. After leading us through numerous corridors, Dora stopped in front of a tall, ebony door and inserted a skeleton key into an iron lock. "I suggest you start in the back."

Dora pointed to the far wall of the room and walked away, clearly shaken. Bain and I walked into the cavernous room. Shelves upon shelves were lined with books on any subject relating to magic imaginable.

"Now I know why this library is so ginormous!" I exclaimed.

Bain nodded. "Shall we?"

"Let's do this."

MINDMAGE

We tore through hordes of hardbacks. Pages flipped feverishly past spells of no use. Pimple potion? Pointless. Will of Wolves? Worthless. Underwater Umbrella? Useless. Towers of books topped the table, waiting for us to discover the secrets within. My head swam, but I kept grabbing books and reading.

Hours passed. We wandered the room, reading the titles of books like *Curses of Nixe, Horrible Hexes,* and *Fantasma's Secrets.* The endless options and passing time made my stomach lurch. An anxious silence filled the room with its weight. *What if we don't find anything?* I thought. *So many people, living and dead, are counting on us. And at the end of our lives, we'll regret it if we can't fix this.*

I continued searching through the old parchment pages. I felt ready to give up when I read something that made my heart skip a beat. Page 443 of *Madame Looney's Magic Guide* read:

Seeking Spell
If what you seek is near
and yet you cannot find it
shout out for all to hear
"*(name of item) to me submit!*"
And within arm's reach, it will appear.

I looked at Bain, his long black hair falling into his eyes as he read with an intensity I admired. But I really didn't want to look silly in front of him. What if I yelled out, telling the spell to come to me and nothing happened? I'd look crazy. *All of this looks crazy. I may as well risk it,* my internal voice encouraged me.

I sighed, stood up, and shouted, "The *Curse of Trapped Souls* to me submit!" Bain looked up, jaw gaping. My heartbeat quickened as Bain's confusion became more and more apparent. I searched the room, silently praying that something would happen.

"What are you..." Bain began, but before he could form his question, a blue leather volume blew by his head and bounced onto the table in front of me. It opened, the pages flipping, then stopped abruptly.

Almost afraid to look, I broke eye contact with Bain and turned to the book. Biting my lip, I read the first line on the page. I looked up, unable to form words.

We had found the curse.

The Curse of Trapped Souls
To forever bind the souls of your enemies
to a single spot,
gather the following necessities
and begin your plot.
Hair of mermaid,
lavender root,
sacred berries (also known as fairy's fruit),
four drops of ginger beer
three tulips,
a single unicorn's tear,
and a pinch of rosehips.
Set aside the mermaid's hair.
Mix together the rest.
Name your enemy seventy-two times as you mix.
Speak into the bottle the place you wish to trap them.

One must journey to the place you want to entrap your enemy.
Set your boundaries, empty the bottle, and leave the mermaid's hair on top.
When what's done is done, the soul of your enemy will never leave.

We barely drew breath as we read the curse over and over again, hoping to understand what to do next. Finally, I broke the silence.

"'What's done is done' must mean death. Lavina must have misunderstood that."

Bain nodded. "She must have named her enemy as anyone who ever walked through the gates of Tansy. She was angry." He shook his head and pulled a notebook out of his backpack. "These books can't leave this room. We'll have to copy it down. Maybe now that we know exactly what went into the spell, your grandma or my parents or someone will know how to break it."

I agreed and watched as Bain copied each word carefully. We couldn't make a single mistake with this spell. There was too much at stake. After we'd double-checked the copy, we carefully put the books away and sent Bain's mom a text to ask her to pick us up.

We stopped at the desk and told Dora about our success. Bain handed her the sheet of notebook paper on which we'd written the spell.

"Do you know how to break this?" he asked.

"Let's see," she said, hope apparent in her voice.

Her eyes darted back and forth as she read the curse several times. After a few moments, her eyes lifted, and she shook her head as sorrow washed over her face.

"I don't know how to break this," she said, barely above a whisper, "but someone will. Someone has to." The old mage's voice lacked the confidence her words portrayed.

My heart sank as we made our way out of the library through the tall, ornate doors. My stomach churned as I realized that even Dora didn't know what to do. Taking in a breath of fresh air to calm my nerves, I spotted a wooden bench beneath a birch tree in a grassy area next to the building. We strolled over to it and sat down. Our hands bumped as we found our places on the bench. I felt my face redden. Again. But I noticed that Bain's cheeks turned a bit pink as well. I didn't have time to focus on my embarrassment because before I could even think of something to say to Bain, Tara Gleason and Holly Penterbrook were standing in front of us, arms overflowing with shopping bags from the nearby boutique. I groaned internally.

"Why would you spend your time with Gross Grace, Bain? I know you're a weirdo, but you're not gross, are you?" Tara teased.

"A girl of substance is never gross, but a shell of a human who only belittles those around her—she is disgusting," Bain replied.

"Did you just call her a disgusting shell?" Holly demanded, pointing a finger at Bain.

"Bain, I'd consider how you talk to me. I decided early on that Grace was a loser, and the rest of the school listened to me. They always do." She smiled and tossed her long blonde hair as she spoke. "If I tell them that you're as gross as she is, they'll all treat you as terribly as they treat Grace." A hateful smirk spread across her face.

Bain shrugged. "I'm not worried."

"And what, you just let your only friend speak for you, Grace?" Tara tapped her pink- polished nails along the arm of the bench.

"I've had nothing to say to you since the second grade, Tara," I replied, turning my head away from her.

Second grade was the year that Tara began to call me Gross Grace and convinced most of our small school to do the same. Second grade was the worst year I had spent in Tansy School, and years later, thinking back to that time still stung.

"Whatever. You're such a freak. And I figured out why you weirdos spend so much time together. My dad told me that, as a kid, he went to the field at the end of town, and he saw *your* grandmother at a weird hippie party with *your* mom and dad." She nodded to me and Bain respectively as she mentioned our families. "What kind of hippie freaks hang out in fields in the middle of the night? My dad says that your crazy families practice weird religious beliefs. Clearly, you two were raised by freaks, and their freakishness wore off on you. You're destined to be losers together." She leaned in, mere inches from my face as she spat the last few words.

So, she knows about the gathering. And it gives her yet another reason to hate us.

"I don't know what your dad thought he saw, but there's nothing freaky about our families," Bain replied.

Tara noticed the tight grip I had on the piece of paper in my hand. She reached for it, trying to take it from me. I clutched the copy of the curse tightly.

"What do you have here, Gross Grace? Something weird, I'm sure." Tara laughed. "Look, Holly, she doesn't want me to see it! It must be a secret love note between the freaks."

Holly let out a cackle and grabbed for the curse as well, her ponytail swishing as she lunged forward. Both girls grabbed and groped at me. Their wild hands blocked me from seeing or even standing up. Rage filled my small frame.

"Stop! Leave her alone!" Bain yelled.

"Aww, look how her boyfriend defends her. Freaks in love!" Tara taunted.

I began to shake with an anger I didn't realize I possessed. This wasn't some silly love note. It was information we needed to save all of the souls of Tansy. Even terrible Tara and her horrible friend, Holly. This was so much more important than these idiotic girls were capable of understanding.

"You. Will. Leave. Us. Alone. Now." I seethed.

To my surprise, the girls turned and walked away without another word. My shock was so great that my mouth hung open. Bain turned to his me and asked, "Are you a mindmage too?"

"I don't know. I don't know how I did that. Or if I did that. What's a mindmage?" I asked.

"A mage with mind control powers. It's uncommon, but then

again, you're a spirittalker with telekinetic ability, so it's safe to say you're a rare bird, Grace," Bain explained, his voice filled with admiration. He rested his hand on my still-shaking shoulder.

"Maybe I am? I was desperate for her to leave. It was like every bit of my body willed her to go," I replied, unsure of myself, but flattered by Bain's praise. I thought back to the first day of summer when my dad seemed to leave the porch by my will. Maybe I did have some sort of mind control powers. The thought sent a shiver down my spine.

Before we could discuss it further, Mrs. Bello pulled up in her black car and honked the horn. We got in the car and immediately told Mrs. Bello that while we didn't have a counter curse, we did have the original spell. I handed her the copy of the curse to inspect.

She read slowly, inspecting every word. Finally, she looked up and spoke. "I don't know how to break this, but this is a great start. I know it doesn't feel like it, but you kids have made a lot of progress. I think you should take it to your grandmother, Grace."

I nodded, trying not to be too disappointed that the two adult mages who'd seen the curse were unable to break it. What chance did I have if all of the adults around me didn't know what to do?

"So, can I take you kids for ice cream?" Mrs. Bello asked.

We weren't about to turn down ice cream. The outing lifted our spirits a bit. I adored spending time with Bain, just talking and having fun. All of the time we'd spent together had been in school or searching through old spell books, so it was nice to just hang out. The break was exactly what I needed.

UPSIDE-DOWN

I found Mom sitting on the front porch feeding lettuce to a wild rabbit when I walked up the driveway. Upon seeing me, the little brown bunny scampered off into the bushes. Animals loved my mom, but the only one that liked me was Midnight. And he was dead, so I wasn't sure if that counted.

"How are you walking?" Mom gasped.

"Mrs. Bello is a healer. She came over this morning and fixed my leg. It hurt really bad, but now it's back to normal, so I guess it was worth it," I explained.

Mom shook her head. "A *healer*. It's like the whole world's been turned upside down."

"It is, isn't it? We were part of a world we knew nothing about all our lives, and we're just now finding out about it," I said, putting my hand on Mom's shoulder. We hadn't been able to have an in-depth conversation about everything happening to us. Mom had been covering for another nurse who was on maternity leave, and all of the extra shifts meant she wasn't home much. Eager to have a chance to talk, I sat down in the white rocking chair next to my mom. I was about to tell her all about my day when I became aware of several spirits surrounding me.

I love you guys, but not now, I thought.

Thomas Meyer appeared between my mom and me.

"Any news?" he asked, hope filling his ghostly voice.

Bartholomew Foster's eyeless face popped up next to Thomas. Polly Hansen perched on the porch rail, watching anxiously. Jenni called hello from the tire swing hanging from the willow tree in my front yard. Before I could speak, another group of ghosts appeared on the steps. I would have to explain it to Mom and the ghosts at the same time.

"We went to the library in Omyra," I said, looking at Mom, but knowing that the ghosts would also benefit from the conversation. "The head librarian is a mage. She keeps a secret room full of magical books. A gigantic room bigger than our house."

"Did you find anything useful?"

I nodded, pulled out the curse, and handed it to Mom. "We found the original curse."

Mom smoothed out the sheet of paper, still wrinkled from my encounter with Tara. She read it silently for a few minutes.

"I wish I knew how to help," Mom finally said. "Maybe Grandma Gertrude will know."

"Maybe," I said. "I'll go inside and call her." I paused for a moment as I opened the front door. I was disappointed that I'd lost my chance to have a deep discussion with my mom. Sympathetic to the ghosts' desperation, I still wished for a moment of peace.

Grandma wasn't home, but I left a message, explaining what we'd found and hoped that she would know what to do. Midnight waited for me in my room, sitting on top of a stack of canvases. A smile stretched across my face as he floated over to me.

"Hi, Kitty-Cat!" I greeted him warmly. "I missed you today."

Midnight meowed at me and rubbed against my leg. Time alone with Midnight was what I needed to clear my mind after the day I'd had. I settled in on my bed and called the ghost cat over.

Unfortunately, the other ghosts of Tansy had other plans. After only a few moments, my room teemed with spirits demanding answers.

"What's your next move?" Polly asked.

"Do you think your grandmother knows how to break the spell?" Thomas chimed in.

An old spirit by the name of Stella Silver spoke up. "What good is having a copy of the curse if you don't know how to break it?" Stella was a pessimistic old woman who had been crabby every time I encountered her. When she was alive, she had been just as grouchy, or so some of the other ghosts had said.

I let out a frustrated sigh. "I don't know. I don't know what to do next, I don't know if Grandma will know either, and I'm really not sure if knowing what's in this curse will make a difference." I shot a look at Stella, who huffed and disappeared. "But I can tell you all that I am trying. Bain is trying. Grandma will help however she can. We all want to help you."

"We know you want to help. I'm sorry if we seem pushy," Polly apologized. "We've been waiting for so long. We're excited, that's all."

"I know you're doing your best, Grace. If we can help somehow, you've got thousands willing to do what we can," Thomas added.

"Our gratitude is great. You've been through..." Bartholomew began. As he spoke his words lost volume, and his appearance faded away until his eyeless face was no longer visible. He was gone.

My heart sank. "Does he normally fade?" I asked Polly.

She shook her head. "That's the first time I've seen."

"Is it affecting more of you than before?" I asked the group of ghosts.

Polly looked away. Thomas floated closer to her, wrapping his smoky arms around his friend. "It happened to Polly twice yesterday."

"Oh, Pol." I suppressed the urge to break down into a sob. "I will fix this. I promise you all. Nothing will stop me from breaking this curse. I've got to get back to work."

With that, they bid me goodbye, then disappeared. I was alone with Midnight again, which gave me comfort. This, however, was short-lived. After only a few moments of silence, Mom knocked on the door of my bedroom.

"Grandma's downstairs," she said from the hallway.

I hopped off my bed, surprised by this news. "She's here? I didn't know she was coming," I replied as I opened the door.

"She said she heard your message and drove straight here. She's hoping something in the curse will let her know what you need to do to break it."

Mom and I didn't speak as we meandered down the stairs, both of us lost in thought. I prayed silently that Grandma would be able to come up with a plan to crack the curse.

Grandma stood in the center of the living room, her jaw set. Her blue eyes lacked their usual flicker of joy. Grandma had her game-face on.

I greeted her as I reached for the curse in my pocket. "Am I right to assume that you'd like to read this?"

Grandma nodded and took the crumpled curse from my hands.

"You only found this information this afternoon, and it's already in a state of disarray?" Grandma said from under furrowed eyebrows.

"Tara Gleason tried to take it. It got a bit crinkled in the process."

"Gleason? Is that Edward Gleason's granddaughter? He was an uptight stick-in-the-mud if I ever met one."

"I'm not sure, but Tara's not especially pleasant, so probably."

"The Gleason family has been unkind to our people for generations. I would not recommend associating with her."

"Trust me, Grandma, I try my hardest to avoid her." *That's the understatement of the century.*

She turned back to the curse and read it. She sat on the sofa and scoured the page a second time. She squinted, pulled her reading glasses out of her large lavender bag, and read it a third time. She pursed her lips, shook her head, and occasionally bit her lip as she read.

"This is dark, dark magic," she finally said. "Not at all the kind of witchcraft Lavina was known for. I wish I knew a counter-spell off hand, but I don't. The ingredients she used are potent. I haven't studied witchcraft, especially not this type. But I do know someone who has."

"Who?" Mom asked from across the room. Mom's silence until this point caused me to forget she was there.

"Your Aunt Gillian. It looks like a road trip is in order."

I had met my Great-Aunt Gillian only a handful of times. She lived three hours away and didn't like to travel. She and Grandma were not especially close from what I gathered. I remembered her as a stern woman who seldom laughed, but she had always been civil, if not kind, to me.

"We should go soon. The ghosts are fading more frequently. I'm afraid we're running low on time." I tried my best not to cry, but tears escaped from my eyes and slid down my cheeks.

"Let me make a phone call," Grandma replied. "But I would like to leave tomorrow morning if that's okay with you, Gabby."

Mom nodded her agreement. "I have some time off work this weekend anyway," she said. "Jane's first day back after maternity leave is tomorrow."

Grandma excused herself to call her sister on the front porch. She returned a few minutes later, her face filled with determination. "It's all set. Gillian said she would do whatever she can to help. I've spoken to my next-door neighbor, and she's promised to look in on Grandpa. I will be here tomorrow at 8:00 to pick you two up."

Grandma said her goodbyes, and I decided to head to bed. I hadn't even made it up the stairs before a gaggle of ghosts found me and begged for information on Gillian. I didn't know much and left the spirits disappointed before I crawled under the covers.

A REALLY CREEPY HOUSE

The next morning, we packed bags for our overnight stay. I sent Bain a text to update him on the situation. He replied, *Thanks for keeping me in the loop. I had a good time with you at the library yesterday. See you when you get back to Tansy.*

I beamed, my grin so wide that my jaw ached. He liked spending time with me! I slipped my phone back into my pocket just as Grandma Gertrude honked her horn, letting us know it was time to go. I gave Dad a quick hug, Mom gave him a kiss, and we ran out the door. Midnight sat on the porch, floating above a pot of petunias.

"Bye, Kitty. See you soon, okay?" He mewed, sounding annoyed. "I promise, I'm only going to be gone a day or two." I laughed.

He meowed loudly and walked up to the car. He hopped through the closed door and sat on the seat. It seemed we had a stowaway.

I turned to explain the cat's presence to my mom, but before I could speak, spirits materialized all around me.

"Thank you, Grace, for doing this for us," Thomas told me.

"Have a safe trip," Polly added.

Several of the other spirits whispered words of support as I situated myself in the backseat of Grandma's gray sedan. Bartholomew and Mrs. Mooney floated right up to the car window and hovered alongside as we pulled out of the driveway, their faces right up against the glass. My chest swelled with emotion. These ghosts were my closest friends. I was going to miss them when we broke the curse.

If we can break the curse.

If not, I'd lose them anyway, to whatever fate they faced when they faded away forever.

I gazed out the window as Mom and Grandma chatted about Great-Aunt Gillian. As much as living in a tiny town like Tansy could be hard, I appreciated the colorful vistas and the breathtaking landscapes that the Fantasma Mountains offered. I gazed at the purple peaks, the kaleidoscopic fields of wildflowers, and the sparkling azure waters of Lake Nixie, mesmerized by the beauty that was my everyday life.

Grandma's car twisted down the windy road leading out of the mountains, the air thick with anticipation. All I could think of was breaking the curse. I prayed that Great-Aunt Gillian's experience with dark witchcraft would be enough to break a three-hundred-year-old curse.

I eventually drifted off into a deep sleep. The car jerked and I woke, startled. We'd arrived at Gillian's house. I stretched my sleepy arms and yawned.

"We're here, Gracie," Mom said. "Grab your bag, and let's go inside."

I looked back to the old Victorian house, taking note of the black paint, shingled roof, spired towers, and crooked shutters. I got out of the car, grabbed my backpack from the trunk, and patted the air where Midnight stood. We walked down a crooked cobblestone pathway to the front porch, which was coated with peeling gray paint. A dead fern sat in a black pot next to a black welcome mat.

The place looked like a haunted house from a picture book. I kept my criticism and reservations to myself. It was too late to turn back now. I hoped that my great aunt was just not into home maintenance. Grandma picked up the rusted iron knocker and rapped the door three times. Within seconds, it creaked open to reveal Great-Aunt Gillian.

"Hello, dearies," Gillian chirped. She reached her wrinkled hands toward me and wrapped me up in a tight hug. I tried not to flinch, but I'm pretty sure I failed. I hadn't expected such warmth from my great aunt. I certainly hadn't experienced it in the past. Decorum, yes. Love? No.

She released me, and her demeanor darkened. "Come in. You can put your bags by the door for now," she instructed, waving her arm, which was covered in a black lace sleeve to match the gown she wore, to the right side of the dark foyer. We obeyed the old mage's order.

"Follow me to the kitchen. I've made tea." Gillian forced a tight smile onto her thin lips. She snapped around toward the back of the house and expected us to follow. The living did. Midnight, however, floated off to explore the house.

I despised tea, however, I didn't tell Gillian this. I didn't get the feeling that my aunt would keep a fridge filled with soda, or that she would offer it to me even if she did. Gillian led us down a dark, cobweb-filled hallway toward the back of the house. I eyed the paintings on the wall, all filled with spooky scenes wrapped in swirling silver frames. Some of the images shot shivers down my spine. One depicted a dozen demonic dogs running rabidly toward a screaming man. Another pictured a woman weeping. The third, the one I found the creepiest, showed children sitting in a cemetery staring at the frame's edge as they gazed into the soul of the viewer. The children, like Bartholomew Foster, had no eyes.

Why would anyone put these in their home?

I turned my focus back to Gillian, who smiled as she chatted with Grandma about a peculiar plant she'd put in pots around the house to ward off gnomes.

"Why do you want to keep gnomes away?" I asked.

Until that moment, I assumed gnomes were something one only found in fairy tales and not in the spooky home of my great aunt.

Gillian burst out laughing. "Why? Child, don't you know anything about our world? Gnomes are nasty little creatures," she said, leaning in so her dark eyes were level with my own. "They'll eat you out of house and home and destroy your hardwoods if you let them."

"Oh," I replied in a voice barely above a whisper. I wasn't used to adults laughing at me for asking what I considered to be a perfectly reasonable question.

Gillian realized she'd hurt my feelings. "I'm sorry, child. I know you weren't raised as a mage." She shot Grandma a look that let me know that my great aunt didn't approve of Grandma's choice to keep magic out of Mom's life all those years ago.

Grandma's eyes misted a bit. The pain on her face was palpable. My gut sank with empathy for my grandma. I put my hand on her shoulder, trying to let her know that I forgave her.

"She's learning quickly. Making up for lost time," Grandma replied in my defense.

Gillian only nodded her head slightly in response.

When we finally reached the kitchen of the maze-like house, Gillian waved her hand to the table, set with tea and biscuits. I pulled a black chair out away from the matching table and sat down. I inspected the berry biscuit on the black plate set before me. It was as solid as a stone. I picked at it politely as the others chatted. I hoped Gillian wouldn't realize that I wasn't actually eating the disgusting pastry.

For the first hour or so, the adults talked, and I listened. Occasionally, someone would ask me a question or include me momentarily in the conversation, but, for the most part, I was left alone with my thoughts. And Midnight, who purred beside my feet the whole time. I shifted in my chair as my stomach churned. We'd come so far to solve this mystery, and I wanted to get started.

"What's wrong, child?" Gillian eventually asked.

"I'm just anxious to get to work. I'm sorry," I replied.

"Well. You're a motivated little mage, aren't you?" Gillian's wrinkled face twisted into a smile.

I nodded, trying not to let it bother me that my great aunt kept calling me "child" and "little."

"I suppose it's time to head up to the library," Gillian declared as she stood, smoothing the lace on her dress. "To the tower."

DON'T CALL ME CHILD

Up in the tallest tower of the creepy house, we worked by candlelight. Of course the tower wasn't wired for electricity. Entering this spooky house was like entering another dimension. Gillian stored her own library of magical texts in the drab, windowless room. Tall black bookcases filled the walls. Stacks and stacks of books lay before us on a solid oak table. Usually, I loved reading, but by this point, I was downright sick of paging through thick, orderless volumes. Futility weighed on my soul.

Gillian, however, did seem to have an idea of how things were organized, and which books might be a good place to start. It was a bit less overwhelming than the library in Omyra had been.

A multitude of books on magical topics was piled precariously before each of us. We chatted quietly about anything we thought might have merit. We passed the copy of the curse Bain made in the library back and forth. Gillian took a lot of notes. I almost felt like I was sitting in school instead of my great aunt's creepy house.

After three hours, it was late, and our eyes were weary. Gillian said that it was time to break for the night. I was grumpy. I'd imagined a lively chat with Gillian leading to a quick discovery. In reality, it wasn't that simple. Gillian explained that while she studied dark witchcraft and owned quite the collection of books on the matter, she had never hexed anyone. It was an interest, not a habit, and her knowledge was limited.

Tired or not, I wasn't ready to give up on my quest. I spotted a book on the bottom of a stack. Gillian had made a pile of books she said she thought wouldn't be of use to us. The title on the book on the bottom of her pile caught my attention. *Breaking the Dark Curse.* That's exactly what we wanted to do, wasn't it? I walked across the room and grabbed the gray book.

"It's time for you to head to bed, Grace," Gillian barked in a stern voice.

Exhausted, I grunted my protest instead of speaking. I opened the book and sat back down. I paged through the book in a frenzy. I felt a pull to a certain page.

175, a voice within me spoke. *Page 175 is what you need.* I tried to remain calm as I flipped to the correct page. It was probably exhaustion speaking to me, not a helpful guide.

When I arrived on page 175, I gasped. This seemed to be exactly what we needed. It read:

When a curse is cast with mermaid's hair
one must break it with the same.
In addition, you need something rare—
a fairy's middle name.

"Wait. Look. I think I found something!" My heart pounded in my chest. Gillian rose and walked over to me. Mom and Grandma watched silently, mouths open and eyes wide as the old mage read over my shoulder. Midnight meowed loudly.

"I think you're right, dear. You've found something indeed." She didn't sound especially happy, but I thought that maybe she was just as tired as the rest of us.

Midnight purred and rubbed against my ankles. A smile spread across my lips for a moment before doubt crept back into my thoughts and snatched away my hope.

"Where do we get mermaid hair? And what do they even mean by a fairy's middle name?"

"Those are worries we can save for tomorrow, child. This is a great discovery to be celebrated. Let's go have pie in the parlor before we slumber."

I wanted to protest but thought better of it. Besides, my stomach ached with hunger, and pie sounded pleasant. Then again, pie always sounded pleasant. Gillian grabbed the book from my hands, and everyone headed down the rickety stairs, past the creepy canvases, and into the parlor. Gillian excused herself and came back with cherry pie a few minutes later. I tried to savor the moment. There would be time in the morning to figure out the rest.

And anyway, the pie certainly was tastier than the biscuits. I suspected it was store-bought.

"I'll wash the dishes," I offered when the pie was finished. I hoped that acting responsible might make Gillian quit calling me child.

"That's sweet, Grace. Thank you," Mom said. "I think I'll head up to bed now." Mom hugged me, handed over her plate, and exited the room.

"Yes, thank you, honey. Goodnight, Grace. Goodnight, Gillian." Grandma gave me her plate and followed Mom.

"Goodnight, child," Gillian said as she left the room.

So much for that, I grumbled internally.

I let out a sigh and walked around the table, gathering the remaining dishes. Midnight appeared, floating around my ankles. I greeted my cat and lugged the heavy stack of plates into the kitchen and set them next to the sink. Lost in thought, I'd nearly completed the task of cleaning the dishes when a voice startled me.

"You'll never be much of a mage, you know."

I turned to see my great aunt standing in the doorway, a black bathrobe wrapped around her small frame. Midnight hissed.

"Wha—excuse...um..." I stuttered, too shocked to form a complete thought.

"That mother of yours is talentless after a lifetime of neglecting her abilities. And my sister, too ashamed of who she is to practice magic openly for decades? The two of them are a disgrace to mages everywhere. *They* are supposed to guide you, child? You who did not know who you were for almost thirteen years? I don't care what you found in that book tonight. The three of you are not capable of breaking a curse." She practically spit her words at me.

"I...I want to try. The curse..."

"I wouldn't bother, child. You should forget about magic. It's not for everyone. Especially not the granddaughter of a traitor like my sister."

With that, she turned around and left the kitchen. I stood in shock for a few minutes, gloved hands dripping soap bubbles onto the dark stone floors. Eventually, with a feeling of unease in my belly, I removed the gloves, neglected to finish washing the dishes, and headed to bed.

I WOKE up the next morning with Midnight at my feet. I looked around the room and jumped a bit when I found a ghost waiting for me. Excluding my ghostly pet, I hadn't seen a single spirit since leaving Tansy.

"Who are you?" I asked the wispy white woman in the corner.

"I'm your great grandmother, Genevieve. I've come to warn you."

"Warn me? Warn me of what?" I whispered, afraid.

"Gillian. She doesn't want you to break the curse."

"I got that feeling last night. She doesn't seem to like me. But I found that passage..." I began.

"She never intended for that to happen. Your great aunt harbors hostility toward your grandmother and, by proxy, to you and your mother. She does not want you to succeed."

"But why? Why does she dislike us so much?"

My great grandma floated closer to me. "She never forgave her sister for turning her back on our ways."

"But she's been to Tansy. She grew up there! This curse will affect her, as well." A realization came over me. "And why aren't you in Tansy? Shouldn't this curse affect you too?"

"It should. You are not the first girl in our family to be a spirtttalker. My great-great-grandmother was as well. She was not as strong as you are. Your powers for communicating with the dead are stronger than any I've ever heard of. She never could see spirits. She sensed their presence and heard some whispering. She lived in Lavina's time. She sensed the souls piling up in Tansy, unable to leave. She did not know what had happened, but she cast a protection spell over all of the Mages of Nixie and their descendants. We are all safe."

"If you've known this, why didn't Grandma know?"

"Shortly before my death, I told Gillian everything. I begged her to share the information with your grandmother, but when Gertrude turned her back on magic, Gillian became enraged and refused to tell your grandmother anything. She's been practicing dark magic ever since. She'd rather see the three of you struggle than help you."

"She said it was just an interest, that she didn't practice dark magic," I replied, my voice cracking.

"That's what she tells people, Grace, but it's not true. She's done terrible things." The old ghost moaned, her face twisted into a pained expression.

"So what do I do? I remember the passage. I need mermaid's hair and a fairy's middle name. But I have no clue how to get either."

"Go back to Tansy, Grace. You'll find your answers with your friends."

"My friends? Bain? The ghosts?"

"You'll see, my dear," the spirit smiled.

"Okay," I said tentatively. "What do I say to Great-Aunt Gillian?"

"Don't let her know that you're on to her. She's dangerous. And Grace? It was a pleasure meeting you." The spirit's milky eyes shone with pride.

With that, the wispy woman wafted away. I looked at Midnight. "Things have been weird lately, Kitty-Cat."

Midnight looked right into my eyes and meowed his agreement.

I threw on my clothes, filled my backpack, and headed down the stairs toward the kitchen where I could hear Mom and Grandma talking. I didn't hear Gillian's voice.

I wonder if I can use magic to convince them like I did with Tara at the library, I mused. *The only problem is I have no clue how I did that!*

I sat down at the table. Mom greeted me with a hug. Both Mom and Grandma seemed so cheerful. They were enjoying the time spent at Gillian's house. *If only they knew,* I thought.

I remembered how furious I'd felt at the library with Tara. Maybe rage had something to do with my power. I certainly was angry with my great aunt for trying to trick me. After the spirit of my great grandmother explained to me that Gillian tried to hide the information from us, it made sense. She'd hidden the book on the bottom of a stack and kept it close to her. She convinced us all to go to bed after we found the passage. She wasn't trying to help us rest—she was trying to distract us. And that rude encounter in the kitchen! The more I thought about it, the angrier I got, and as my rage increased, it became clear to me what to do.

I stood, looked at my mom and grandma, and spoke. "It's time to leave," I said, each word slow and deliberate. They complied.

"It's time to leave," they agreed in unison.

"Go get your bags." I kept my tone steady.

They nodded and left the room. A moment later, Gillian came into the kitchen. Rage flooded through me like never before.

"Where is everyone?" she asked in a sugary tone.

"They've gone to get their bags," I replied, keeping my tone as calm as I could. "It's time we left."

"Oh, no, you don't need to leave."

It's not working. Why isn't it working? My mind raced.

"We. Are. Leaving," I looked at her with a fiery intensity.

"No. Stay. Have some tea, child."

Child? CHILD? I will not allow this horrendous woman to call me child any longer!

"I don't *like* tea. We. Are. Leaving." I gazed at my great aunt, unwilling to break eye contact.

"Do you really think you can mindmage me, child?"

A jolt of shock shot through me, but I held my ground.

"I can, and I will. Gillian, we are going home. You will not stop us," I said, my voice holding steady as I panicked internally.

There was a painfully long silence, then suddenly, Gillian's eyes glazed over and her jaw relaxed. "It's time for you to leave," she said, the tone of her voice detached.

"Yes," I agreed, heart racing.

Minutes later, we began our trip back to Tansy. An ache filled my stomach as the car wound down the twisty road, but I wasn't carsick. Guilt and fear bubbled around in my belly. I knew I had to tell them what I knew. And what I did.

"Mom, Grandma. I met Great-Grandma Genevieve this morning."

"You what?" Confusion rang through Mom's voice.

"Great-Grandma visited me this morning. She was waiting for me when I woke up. She told me some things that I think I need to tell you."

"Oh, how I wish I could have your powers from time to time," Grandma mused, her voice full of longing.

"It was special to meet her, but that's not what I'm trying to tell you. She told me some things about Great-Aunt Gillian. And the curse."

The silence that followed was palpable.

"Great-Aunt Gillian doesn't like any of us. In fact, she hates us. She doesn't want us to succeed in breaking the curse."

"Oh, no, dear. I know my sister is not the cheeriest woman ever, but she doesn't hate us. While she may be crabby, Gillian herself will be cursed if you're not successful."

"But that's the thing. She won't be cursed. None of us will be. Generations ago, there was a spirittalker in our family. She couldn't speak to spirits the way I can, but she was able to sense their presence. She didn't know exactly what had happened, but she felt the ghosts piling up in town and cast a spell of protection over the Mages of Nixie. We're all safe. And so is Gillian. Great-Grandma told her this, and she was supposed to tell you, but she didn't. And there's more. Those books on dark magic are not just there because she has an interest in it. She's been practicing it for years. Great-Grandma said that she's dangerous and that we needed to get away from her."

I could see Grandma's shoulders tense up. After a moment, I continued to speak. "Great-Grandma told me that Gillian hates you because you quit practicing when Mom was born. And she hates Mom and me because we're close to you. Great-Grandma seemed worried for us all. So I made sure we left."

"Made sure? How?" Mom asked.

"Well. I can do this thing. I've only done it a few times. Bain calls it mindmaging."

"Wait. You're a mindmage?" Grandma covered her mouth with her hand.

"Apparently."

"And you used that power on us?"

"Yes. And on Gillian. But only to get us out of that house before she realized that I knew she wasn't on our side."

"What does that mean, mindmage?" Mom asked.

"I can persuade people to do things. With my mind."

"That's not a power for you to take lightly, Grace." Tension flowed from Grandma in waves.

"I know. And I don't. I normally wouldn't have used it. But I was so scared for all of us. And there wasn't time to explain." I hoped Mom and Grandma would understand.

"While I'm not fond of being mindmaged, let alone by my own granddaughter, I understand," Grandma finally said.

We rode in silence for a few miles. Suddenly, Mom spoke.

"Grace, please don't ever do that to me again, unless you have to."

"Of course."

"And Grace?" Mom said, meeting my eyes in the rear view mirror.

"Yeah, Mom?" I replied, shifting in my seat.

"Thank you."

"You're welcome."

Most of the drive was quiet. At least an hour passed without anyone speaking a single word aloud. The weight of the danger we just missed hung in the air. Eventually, Grandma spoke up in a strained voice.

"I fear my sister may retaliate when she realizes that you've used your mindmage powers on her."

Adrenaline pulsed through me. I hadn't even thought about that. Why did I make the evil mage mad at me? What a stupid move!

"I can put a spell of protection around Tansy to keep her out, but I can't promise it will hold for long. She's powerful, and if she wants to break it, she will. It won't be instant. It could take her months or even years. I pray she moves on when she realizes it will take time. She doesn't like to leave her home, and maybe she'll retreat instead of hold her ground. Maybe," Grandma said, her voice sounding unsure.

"Thank you," I said, feeling a bit safer. Not totally at ease, but I at least felt confident that I would have time to break this curse without Gillian's interference.

More motivated than ever, I tried to work out what my next steps might be. I memorized the passage the night before and planned to talk to the Bellos about it as soon as we made it back to town. As we drove, I decided it didn't need to wait.

I texted Bain: *What do u know about mermaid hair and fairy's middle names?*

Bain: *Don't know about fairies. Will ask Mom. Don't u have a bottle with mermaid hair from Lavina's?*

I almost jumped for joy in the backseat. I'd forgotten about the bottle. I thanked Bain and relaxed in my seat.

I was going to break this curse after all. I looked at Midnight curled up next to me on the seat, and the realization that my success would cause me to lose all of my friends set in.

A tear slid down my cheek as I watched Lake Nixie's gleaming cobalt waters come into view.

BOMBARDED BY GHOSTS

The purple house on Willow Way stood waiting for our return. Upon the pastel porch, seventy-six spirits waited. They crowded the space, all trying to get the best view of the driveway. Some hovered above the porch, while others sat on the wooden swing. A gaggle of ghosts squished themselves up to fit on the steps. All of the ghosts wanted to be able to greet me as soon as I exited the car.

As we pulled into the driveway, the ghosts went absolutely wild. Before I could even open the car door, ghouls bombarded me. So many ghosts spoke at once that I couldn't even understand their words.

"...find anything?"

"What's next?"

"...useful information?"

"...nice trip?"

"...dark witch?"

"...break the curse?"

"I'll deal with you all in a moment," I told them.

This didn't help settle them at all. In fact, the ghosts were so overexcited that Mom and Grandma, and, later Dad and Grandpa, too— said they could hear a buzz and feel vibrations that I knew came from a stampede of spirits. They didn't hear or feel it in the same way

I did, of course, but later, I was told that much of the town wondered what in the world was going on that day.

Mom and Grandma went directly inside, but I hung back to talk to the spirits.

"Please, give me a few moments inside. I want to put my bag away and say hello to my dad and grandpa. It won't take long."

The ghosts grumbled, but I went inside anyway. I went upstairs and put my backpack on my bed, then ran back downstairs to say hello to Dad and Grandpa. I chatted with them, got a drink of water, and headed back outside to speak to the spirits.

I opened the door to find that the number of ghosts had grown. Word of my arrival spread quickly, and now at least three hundred ghouls gathered in the garden. As soon as they saw me, the buzzing of questions began again.

"I can't hear you if you all talk at once," I tried to point out, but it was useless. The ghosts couldn't hear me any better than I could hear them over all the racket.

"I SAID, I CAN'T HEAR YOU IF YOU ALL TALK!" I shouted.

Unfortunately, it was this very moment that Tara happened to walk by my house. To anyone who couldn't see ghosts, it appeared that I was standing in my yard yelling at myself. Tara walked right up to me, eager for an opportunity to torment.

"Talking to your imaginary friends again, Gross Grace?" Tara's smile was as wicked as they come.

Angry heat rushed to my face. "Just practicing for a play. Move along, Tara. You're not wanted here."

"There's no play. It's a small town, Grace. I'd know if there was going to be a play in Tansy. I know everything that happens here."

"There's tons you don't know about the town of Tansy, Tara."

"Like what?"

"Like the reason the hair on your neck is standing up right now. The reason you feel uneasy in the dark. There's a reason you don't like me that goes way deeper than the fact that you think I'm weird. And you'll never understand it because you are not capable."

Tara's eyes grew wide as I spoke, but she tried to shake it off. "Whatever, freak," she sneered. She turned toward the street to saunter away when Thomas floated by and grabbed one of her long, blonde pigtail braids, pulling it to the right, and Jenni grabbed the other, pulling it to the left.

"Don't pull my hair, freak," she barked.

"Tara, I am ten feet away from you," I pointed out. "How on earth could I pull your hair? And you call *me* a freak." I giggled.

Tara ran off down the street and out of sight as quickly as her overpriced brand-name sneakers could carry her.

I burst out into a belly-laugh as Tara disappeared around the corner. The ghosts giggled with me, causing the yard to vibrate again. When everyone calmed down, I spoke again, still wiping tears of glee from my eyes.

"If everyone can quiet down, I have news for you all," I began. The ghosts took a moment to stop laughing and whispering. I waited, tapping my fingers on the porch rail until they composed themselves.

"I don't have all of the answers, but I have a good start. I need the hair of a mermaid and the middle name of a fairy to break the curse. I'm not absolutely sure what I do when I have both of those or how on Earth I find a fairy and convince it to tell me its middle name, but it's more information than I had before I left. I'm getting closer to cracking the curse."

The ghosts let out a joyful sound that reverberated quietly throughout Tansy. After several more minutes of musings, the spirits went their separate ways, and I headed inside to fetch Lavina's bottle of mermaid hair.

Midnight was sitting on my bed when I got to my room. I greeted my best friend with a "Hey Kitty-Kitty," and strolled up to the side table and grabbed the ancient bottle marked "Mermaid Hair." I twisted the old cork out of the bottle and peeked inside.

It was empty. There wasn't a single hair inside the bottle. I held it up to the light, desperately desiring for a hidden hair, but all the bottle held was stale air. I groaned.

"No. No, no, no, no, no, no!" I wailed. "Where in the world I am supposed to get a mermaid hair?" I looked at Midnight, wishing he could help.

Midnight, as usual, only meowed in return. I took my phone from my pocket and texted Bain: *Mermaid hair bottle is a bust. Totally empty. Do u know any mermaids? Haha.*

A moment later, my phone buzzed with his response: *I don't, but I know someone who does. Will text Sophia and get back to u.*

I stared at my phone and thought about how my life had changed in such a short time. A month ago, I didn't even believe in mermaids. Now, I knew someone who knew a mermaid and I didn't even think it was strange. I knew Sophia a bit from school. She was a few years older, but never teased me like most of the others.

Ten minutes later, my phone buzzed again, notifying me of a new text from Bain: *My friend Sophia can help. She and I will be outside your house at 10:30 tomorrow morning.*

OMG, I texted back, *Thanks! See u then!*

MERMAID QUEST

I woke up about ten o'clock the next morning. I showered, dressed in my favorite gray tank top, and flew to the fridge to grab some fruit before heading outside to meet Bain and Sophia.

They hadn't arrived yet, so I plopped down on the purple porch swing and tried to imagine what it would be like to meet a mermaid. As I sat lost in thought, Midnight appeared and meowed loudly at me. I reached my hand down to stroke the cold ghost and felt a lump form in my chest. I couldn't bear the thought of saying goodbye to Midnight. Every step we completed to breaking the curse brought me one step closer to losing my best friend forever.

I didn't have long to dwell on my sadness because Bain and Sophia arrived just then. Bain smiled and waved. Sophia waved and called hello.

I stood, whispered a wistful goodbye to Midnight, and jogged to meet them. "Hey, guys. Thanks for helping me."

"From what Bain tells me, we're helping the whole town," Sophia said. "What a horrible curse!" She shook her head, her short black curls bouncing as she moved.

"It is pretty awful," I agreed.

"I guess we should get to it," Sophia said. I didn't know her well, but she had a reputation for being blunt. Not mean, just to the point.

"We should," Bain agreed.

"Okay," I said. "Where are we going?"

"To the lake, of course." Sophia shot Bain a look that clearly said, *Is this girl for real?*

I tried to fight back the feeling of stupidity that fell over me. I wished that I'd known about the magic that surrounded my town all my life like they had.

We walked toward the north end of town where Lake Nixie dipped into the Fantasma Mountains and formed one edge of the town of Tansy. Lake Nixie was an expansive body of water that went on for miles.

"I never knew there were mermaids in Lake Nixie," I said to the other kids.

"Not many do," Sophia explained. "They don't like to be seen."

"I've never seen one," Bain admitted. He shot a shy smile in my direction.

"So, how do we find one?" I asked, feeling stupid again.

"Sophia's an aquamage. She's connected with the water," Bain explained.

Sophia nodded, clearly proud of her powers. "I can communicate with the creatures in Lake Nixie. I also can move the water how I wish."

"Wow! That's so cool!" I said.

We'd arrived at the shore of the lake next to Tansy's town park. I gazed into the glimmering blue-green waters of the lake I'd seen every day of my life. It had been a magical place all along, and I'd never known. I'd never bothered to consider that there was another world hidden beneath its surface. I remembered Bain's words about the lake being the source of magic. I wondered what else could be down there.

Sophia kneeled on the lake shore and stuck her hand into the water. To my surprise, the water moved away from her dark skin. She stayed dry as the lake formed a divot wherever her hand moved.

"I'm just letting them know we've arrived," Sophia explained.

"And what, they'll pop up and say hello in the middle of the park?" I asked.

"Oh, no." Sophia laughed. "It's not that simple, even for an aquamage."

Sophia stood and strolled along the shore toward an old rickety pier. No one in Tansy had used the decrepit dock in years. When the town built a new one ages ago, it neglected to tear down the old one.

Sophia led us to the far side of the dock, out of the watchful eyes of the parents of Tansy who had brought their kids to play at the park. Sophia looked around to be sure we wouldn't be seen, then plunged her palm into the lake again. The water parted, and up popped a small wooden rowboat which was, inexplicably, as dry as a bone.

"Let's get moving," Sophia instructed. "They don't like to be bothered too late in the day."

Bain hopped into the rowboat, followed by Sophia. I hung back a moment, overwhelmed by the idea of jumping into a boat to meet a mermaid. *How weird is this?* I thought as I took a deep breath and climbed in after the others. Once in the boat, I noticed that there were no oars.

"Don't we need..." I began, but before I could finish my thought, Sophia raised her arm over her head, and the boat glided across the water with ease.

"One of the perks of being an aquamage is that I don't need oars." Sophia chuckled. The smile on her face told me that she took a lot of pride in her powers.

The boat whizzed through the waves, weaving around buoys and winding along the shoreline. The wind stung my face as I breathed in the crisp air and the earthy smell of the mud on the shore. Sophia set her aim for the furthest point from town. After about twenty minutes, the boat came to a stop in a little cove where the lake met the rocky mountains. This area would be difficult, if not impossible, to reach without a boat.

A sprite-like smile spread across Sophia's face. "We're here!"

Bain and I leaned over the edge of the boat, looking into the lake for any signs of mermaids. The water lapped around the boat. Beams of sunlight illuminated the water so that I could just make out the lake's floor. I squinted, straining to see some hint of a mermaid, but I only spied a fish swimming below the lake's surface.

Sophia plunged her arm into the lake. She opened and closed her hand several times. Each time she closed her hand into a fist, a ball of purple water shot out, causing ripples in the lake.

"I'm calling them," she explained. "We'll see who responds. If it's Nix, she'll probably be willing to share a strand of hair without issue. If it's Lorelei, she might be harder to convince. And if it's Nerida, we may as well come back another day. Sometimes they come together, but most often one at a time. They all like me well enough, but they aren't used to strangers. I don't exactly bring people out here. You're actually the only ones I've brought, other than my sister. And Nerida didn't like it when I brought her."

I gulped. I hadn't even thought about the fact that the mermaids might not want to share their hair. Getting to them seemed like enough of a journey. I closed my eyes and hoped that Nix would be the one to answer Sophia's call.

A few moments later, a shimmering silver tail splashed out of the lake. The swimmer dove back down for a few moments, then popped up beside the rowboat. The mermaid's hair matched her silvery tail, and she wore a scowl on her beautiful face. Without asking, I knew this must be Nerida.

"Hello, Nerida," Sophia greeted the mermaid warmly.

"Who have you brought to our sacred cove?" the mermaid snapped in response.

"These are my friends, Bain and Grace. They're mages."

Nerida's eyes were angry slits of emerald green. "Aquamages?"

"No. Bain is an embermage, so he has some water abilities, but he's no aqua. And Grace here is a spirittalker, and she has some other abilities as well." I had a feeling that if Sophia were to mention that I was a mindmage, it would have sent Nerida deep into the darkest part of Lake Nixie.

"Why did you bring them here?" Nerida demanded.

"We actually need a favor. It's not for us, really, but the entire town of Tansy."

"And what do I care of Tansy?"

"Do you care for me at all?" Sophia asked softly. "Every soul in the city is cursed. Long ago, the White Witch of the Wood cursed anyone who ever crossed the town wall to spend their eternity in Tansy. There are thousands of spirits stuck in Tansy."

"And what am I to do?"

"The curse was made with mermaid hair. The only way to break it involves having another strand of hair from one of your people."

"You want my hair?" Nerida seethed, her face contorting into a furious snarl.

"Just a strand," Sophia pleaded. "There's no other way."

"Cursed humans are not of my concern," Nerida barked, and she dove back into the lake. My stomach clenched as if I'd been punched.

"What now?" I asked, barely above a whisper.

"I...I guess we'll have to come back again and ask Nix or Lorelei," Sophia responded, sounding unsure of herself.

A splash startled us, and we turned to see a pink tail pop out of the water, followed by a teal one. The sunlight reflected off their iridescent scales, and I thought I'd never seen anything quite so beautiful before. Soon, two heads popped up with pink and teal curls surrounding their beautiful faces.

"You don't have to come a second time," the teal-haired mermaid said.

"We'll help," the pink-haired one added.

"We can't let all of those souls be trapped in one spot for eternity," the first mermaid said.

The teal-haired mermaid explained with a solemn look on her face. "We were listening under the water. I am so sorry our sister was so horrible to you. She doesn't trust humans. Many years ago, a man learned of the power that our hair holds. He followed Nerida for days, trying to get her hair. Eventually, he pulled her onto his boat and took a large handful of her hair by force. She never got over it.".

"That's horrible!" I gasped.

"It really was. You can't blame her for being distrusting, but we understand that most humans aren't like that." She nodded to the pink-haired mermaid on her side. "I'm Nix." The teal-haired mermaid held out a slender hand to Bain and me. I smiled and shook her hand, and Bain did the same.

"And I am Lorelei." The pink-haired mermaid held out her hand to shake as well.

Nix ran her fingers through her hair for a moment and tugged a teal hair out of her scalp. She winced, and a tear slipped down her cheek.

"Are you okay?" I asked as Nix handed me the hair.

"Losing a hair is painful for us. Much of our power is in our hair, but I am willing to endure pain for Tansy."

"Thank you so much," I told Nix, humbled by her sacrifice. I had only just met Nix, and yet, she was so willing to help Tansy.

"Yes, thank you, Nix," Sophia added.

Bain beamed. "You saved the day."

"You're welcome, young mages. It's time we left. Nerida will be very angry with us. I'm sure I'll see you soon, Sophia."

We called goodbye to the mermaids, who waved and ducked under the lapping waters. Their shimmering tails popped up a final time, then slipped under the surface of the lake and disappeared down into its depths. I took the teal strand and stuffed it in my pocket. Sophia raised her arm above her head once again, and the rowboat burst forward, flying across the lake's surface. Sunlight warmed my skin. The cheerful summer day matched my mood. We let out a few excited whoops as we zipped back to town in the little boat. We had the hair! It seemed as if we had nearly reached our goal. I pushed aside fears of an angry Nerida and creepy Great-Aunt Gillian. I knew I still had a lot to figure out, but the success and sunshine had me feeling happier than I had in a long time.

25 TO FIND A FAIRY

As the boat whizzed toward town, we discussed how we might locate a fairy. None of us had ever met a fairy before. Bain had asked his parents about it, but they didn't know.

"I've kind of been avoiding talking about it all with Grandma Gertrude," I admitted. "I had to use my mindmage powers on her and Mom to get them to leave Great-Aunt Gillian's house."

"Wait, what?" Bain asked.

"You mindmaged your family?" Sophia sputtered.

"I had to. Great-Aunt Gillian had it in for Grandma Gertrude, and I was the only one who knew. My Great-Grandma Genevieve's ghost came to warn me." I spent the next several minutes relaying the story.

"Dang. That's crazy! I guess you had to do it to get them out of there," Bain replied.

I nodded, thinking about the intense time we'd experienced with my great aunt. The only time that she'd really even seemed like she might be a decent human was when she served us pie. Could that pie have been poisoned? I struggled to remember what kind of pie it might be. Was is cherry? Berry? Suddenly, the thought of berries reminded me of something—sacred berries. I realized where we needed to go.

"Bain, remember the spell talking about the sacred berries? It said it's also known as 'fairy's fruit.' And the map...it said that the berries grew in the field on the edge of town."

"So, I guess that's where we're going!" Bain exclaimed.

"Good timing," Sophia added as the boat met the shore. We climbed out of the boat and onto dry land. Sophia raised her hand above her head, and the small rowboat spiraled down to the lake floor.

My mind swirled as we strolled across town. I had walked through that field countless times and had never seen a fairy. What would we do to make it happen now? And how would we convince the fairy to tell us its name?

It was nearing twilight as our trek to the field ended. We slowly walked through the surrounding area, searching the ground with every step. After several minutes of this, we got down on our hands and knees and crawled, intensely inspecting every inch of earth to no avail.

"Here, fairy, fairy, fairy," called Sophia.

"We aren't looking for a lost cat," Bain pointed out.

"Well, I don't know how to call a fairy!" Sophia stood and crossed her arms.

Just then, a lavender light jumped out at me. I held as still as possible, barely breathing for fear that I'd scare the fairy away. I inched toward it as gently as I could.

"Hello, fairy. My name is Grace. I'm a mage and I'd like to talk to you."

The fairy flew toward me. It was a tiny bolt of light in the amethyst twilight sky. It hovered about a foot from me. Everyone stopped moving.

"I'd like to know your middle name, please." I tried to sound as polite as possible.

The tiny woman threw her head back, tossed her purple hair over her shoulder, and laughed wildly. She doubled over, and laughed and laughed and laughed some more. It was a high-pitched, tinkling laughter that reminded me a bit of a bicycle bell. The tiny fairy flew all around our heads, and went off into the forest, giggling as she flew into a green grove of trees. As she flitted out of sight, disappointment washed over me.

"Should we chase it?" Sophia asked, eyebrows raised.

"We may as well try to follow her," Bain said, pushing his long hair away from his eyes.

"Let's go!" I called, sprinting toward the trees.

Bain and Sophia followed behind me, their feet thudding on the soft grass. As I broke through the tree line, the scent of pine wafted to my nose. The little grove was made dark by the tall pines. I strained my eyes, hoping to see a bolt of purple light.

"Can anyone see her?" I panted.

"Can't see a thing," Sophia said.

"Pull out your phones. Maybe we can use them as flashlights," Bain said.

We dug in our pockets and pulled out our cell phones, shining the lights all around the grove. I didn't see anything other than trees, rocks, mushrooms, and one startled squirrel. Frustrated, I knelt down on the forest floor, searching desperately for any sign the fairy was near. Bain and Sophia joined me, crawling on the mossy ground, the lights of their phones darting around the grove.

We went on this way for at least fifteen minutes. Nothing. No fairy. No light. No shimmer. A heavy sigh escaped my lips as I threw my hands up in the air. The sky turned dark, and our frustration mirrored the night, so we decided to head home. My shoulders sagged, and my head hung as we walked down the street.

"I guess I'm going to have to face my grandma after all."

"Good luck," Sophia said as we parted ways. "Let me know if I can help again."

"Thanks again for helping me today."

Bain and I walked in silence toward my house. We turned onto Willow Way and Bain grabbed my hand, pulling me to a stop.

"I just wanted to let you know that I think you're brave," he told me. His eyes glinted in the moonlight under his furrowed brow. "I know your path has not been an easy one. You were thrown into the life of a mage with an intensity not many of us will ever know."

He wrapped his arms around me in a quick hug. A warm happiness filled my core.

"I'll see you soon. Good luck with your grandma."

Once inside, I took the mermaid hair straight up to my bedroom and put it safely in Lavina's empty mermaid hair bottle. It seemed appropriate to use the vial of hair that was used to curse the village to store the curse-breaking strand of hair.

I pulled out my phone and called Grandma. I explained the situation with the fairy. Grandma said she'd come as soon as she could, and an hour later, she arrived.

"Sweetheart," she told me when she walked through the door, "what you need isn't me. What you need is your mother."

"Mom?" I asked, confused.

"Your mother is naturemage. The fairies will listen to her." Grandma's voice was clear and confidant.

"Who's here?" Mom called from the stairs as she made her way toward the living room. "Oh. Hi, Mom! I didn't know you were coming over."

"Grace asked me to. Can we sit down?" Grandma gestured toward the sofa.

Confusion spread over Mom's face, but she nodded her agreement. We all walked over to the sofa and sat.

"So, what's this about?" Mom asked, tension thick in her throat.

"Remember what we found at Great-Aunt Gillian's?" I asked. "About the mermaid hair and the fairy's middle name? Well, I got the mermaid hair."

"Oh! That's wonderful!" Mom interrupted, clapping her hands as she spoke.

"It is. But, when I tried to talk to a fairy, she laughed at me."

"You found a fairy and she laughed at you?" Mom asked, bewildered.

"Yes. She laughed hysterically."

"Well, that wasn't polite of her," she replied, sounding especially motherly.

"Fairies are not polite creatures, generally speaking," Grandma informed us. "They are beautiful and powerful, but not polite."

"So, what do you do now?" Mom asked.

"Well, dear. That's why we need you," Grandma said.

"Me?" Mom's jaw dropped in disbelief.

"Yes, dear. You, the girl who talked to the animals until your mother pushed that idea out of your head. The one rabbits still follow. The naturemage."

"I...I don't know." Mom looked down, wringing her hands. "I'm not sure that I'm what you need."

"Gabby, I know that you spent years trying to understand why you were different, and I made that harder for you instead of easier, but we're faced with a situation where we truly need someone of your ability. Your skills could play a vital role in breaking Tansy's curse."

A pained expression flashed across Mom's face. "I guess, if you really need me, I could try."

I jumped out of my seat and threw my arms around her. "Thank you!" I squealed.

"Let's plan for dawn," Grandma told us. "Fairies are most active at dawn and dusk."

Early the next morning, Grandma returned. We walked the short stretch across town together. Grandma and I chatted as we strolled, but Mom didn't speak. She kept her head down and her arms crossed.

The sunrise lit the field with a fiery glow. Grandma and I walked into the meadow, but Mom held back.

"You can do this, honey," Grandma told her, placing a hand on my mom's shoulder.

Mom nodded, resolute. She walked to the center of the field and lowered herself into the tall green grass. It was as if she was suddenly where she belonged all along. She held her hands out at her sides and closed her eyes, greeting the fairies in the meadow much as she greeted the bunnies in our yard. Her red hair seemed to glow in the sunrise, and she looked more peaceful than I had ever seen her.

A blinding lavender light flashed in the field. Dozens of tiny beams of light swirled all around Mom. Several landed on her outstretched hands. Her mouth fell into a gaping, shocked smile. Tiny twinkling fairies twirled all around her.

"Hello, little friends," she said sweetly. "I hope you're having a good morning."

Mom listened for a moment. Grandma and I gave her space, not wanting to interrupt or scare the fairies away. Grandma gripped my hand and looked into my eyes as if to say, *This is a moment to be celebrated.*

"It's nice to meet you, too," Mom told a magenta fairy that was perched on her shoulder. A moment later she said, "I bet those berries *are* delicious."

She went on chatting with the fairies as if it were as normal as can be. After several minutes, she gently explained Tansy's situation and asked if anyone would mind sharing their middle name. Several fairies flew away in an instant.

One little fairy, however, flew up to her ear and whispered. The tiny woman was barely an inch tall and wore a garment made from a green leaf. She glowed with a twinkling green light as she leaned into Mom's ear. After a moment, Mom grinned gratefully. "Thank you so much, little friend," she told the fairy. "You've helped save the town."

The fairies swirled around my mom for several seconds and scattered. She walked over to us and said, "Esmeralda. Her middle name is Esmeralda."

I had never seen such a look of pride on Mom's face in my entire life. I hugged her tightly. The walk home was triumphant. Mom's fear of her own magic seemed to float away into the sunrise.

Back at home, Grandma and I discussed strategies to use the mermaid hair and fairy's name to break the curse. Grandma brought a collection of books with her that she'd borrowed from a friend. They were all about different methods to break curses. I sighed, realizing that I was yet again tasked with magical research.

"There should be something in here for you," Grandma said, setting the stack of books on the dining table. "I wish I could stay to help, but Grandpa has chemo," she said, her voice cracking.

My stomach panged with remorse. I'd been so busy that I barely thought about Grandpa. I made mental note to be sure to be at his next chemo appointment.

"Send him my love," I told Grandma. "I've got this."

Grandma left, and I settled in with the books. I felt doomed to page through books forever. While a lot of what was in the thick volumes was interesting, none of it seemed to apply to the *Curse of Trapped Souls*.

After a few hours, anxiety began to creep into the back of my mind. What if the answer wasn't in these books? The ghosts were fading more and more. My stomach roiled, and my face burned hot. I couldn't let them down. My head dropped to the table, my soul feeling defeated.

Footsteps squeaked on the tile floor, and I looked up to find Mom standing in the doorway. Her gray eyes were filled with concern.

"What's wrong, Grace?"

"I have to find out how to break the curse. Soon, before the ghosts fade away forever."

"Well, then let me help you." Mom crossed the room and pulled out the chair next to mine. "Honey, I really am sorry that I wasn't there for you."

"I know you've had a lot of work. Mom. It's fine," I said, brushing off the apology.

"No, I'm not talking about recently. Before. Before I knew what you were. What I was. I couldn't face it. I remembered being an odd child and I didn't want that for you. I wanted you to be normal. But what I didn't realize is that you were *better* than normal. You're extraordinary, Grace. Perfect just how you are. I hope we can do more together in the future," Mom's eyes were misty.

"Thanks, Mom. I know that this has all been hard for you. I'm not mad."

Mom put her hand on mine for a moment, then turned her glance to the books in front of her. I watched her pick it up and begin to flip through the pages, her eyes darting all over the pages feverishly. A warm sensation filled my middle. My mom, in spite of it all, truly cared about me.

I went back to the book in front of me. Something caught my eye, and a wave of relief washed over me.

"I think I found it!" I said, my voice a shaky whisper.

Mom stood, reading over my shoulder. I pointed at a passage in the middle of the page.

"See this? It says to break a curse made with mermaid hair, I need to go back to the place where the curse was originally made."

"Do you know where that is?" Mom asked.

I nodded, thinking back to the mirror's memories. "Right at the gate of the old town wall." I looked down, reading on. "I'll need to read these words to break the curse: *Long ago a curse was made, and now is the time for it to end. This town's curse shall fade, and a new era shall begin. With the hair of a mermaid and the middle name of a fairy —Esmerelda I free Tansy from the* Curse of Trapped Souls." I scanned the page, reading the rest of the instructions and summarized them for Mom. "Next, I need to set the hair on the wall. Within a few moments, the trapped souls will be able to move on to the Light." My pulse began to race. "And they'll be gone." I shook my head in disbelief, and tears burned hot in my eyes. I blinked, willing myself not to cry as I tried to comprehend a world without the ghosts.

"I imagine that won't be easy for you, dear," Mom said gently as she placed her hand on mine.

"No, it won't be." I choked back a sob. "I think I need to be alone for a while before I do this, Mom. Thank you for all of your help."

I ran up the stairs. My throat stung and tears fell down my cheeks. I threw open my bedroom door, sprinted to my bed, and hid my head under the heavy quilt. I quickly realized, however, that even under the covers, I wasn't alone. Midnight appeared next to me and meowed.

"How do I say goodbye to you, Kitty-Cat?" I sobbed. "You've been here every single day, and you'll be gone."

The black spirit cat cocked his head to one side, listening intently. He purred and rubbed up against my cheek, sending a cool tingle down my spine.

"Thank you, Midnight. You've always been there for me. When all the kids in school were mean to me, I knew you would be there to help make me feel better. I am going to feel so empty without you."

I pulled the pillow over my face and sniffled. Midnight wouldn't allow me to hide, however, and he hopped on top of the pillow and pawed me playfully.

"Oh, Kitty-Cat. You've always known how to cheer me up."

Just then, Polly appeared at the foot of the bed. I gulped back a sob at the sight of my friend.

"Polly! Oh, Polly!" was all I could say.

"What's wrong?" Polly asked, her gray face filled with alarm.

"It's time. I'm ready to break the curse. But," I sobbed, "I'm going to miss you so much!"

"Oh, Grace. I know. I am going to miss you, too. But it's far past my time. I need to go on into the Light. We all do. Before we fade away forever."

"I know. That's why I'm going to go break the curse. I just...don't want to say goodbye."

Polly looked pained. "I don't either, but it's time. For us and for you. You need to spend your time with the living instead of with the dead."

I looked at my feet and tried to calm my tears.

"And Grace? We should do this now. Thomas faded for almost a full day. Much longer than anyone has so far. I'm afraid if he fades again, it will be too late. This curse needs to be broken now."

My pulse raced. "Okay. Let's do this. I'll be at the old entry to Tansy at sunset."

"I'll tell the others. I love you, Grace."

"Love you like my dead sister," I replied.

Polly placed her translucent hand over mine for a moment, then disappeared, off to spread the world to the other spirits that the curse would be broken at sunset.

I turned back to Midnight. "Will you stay with me until the end?"

The ghost cat looked deep into my eyes and meowed. I knew he'd be with me as long as he could be. A hollow pain hung in my chest. I spent several silent minutes with Midnight before I was ready.

It was time to break the curse of Tansy.

TERRORIZING TARA

Vial of valuable mermaid hair in hand, I made my way across town with Midnight walking at my side and tears streaming down my cheeks. Mom and Grandma offered to go with me, but I knew this was something I needed to do alone.

I spoke to Midnight as we walked. Usually, I tried not to talk to ghosts in public, but I was past the point of caring. It was my last chance to be with him, and I was going to try to enjoy it.

"You've been such a good kitty," I cooed.

"Gross Grace is talking to herself again," laughed a vicious voice.

I looked up to see Tara. *Of course, it's Tara. Just what I needed,* I thought as the bully sauntered up, hands on her hips.

"Leave me alone, Tara," I growled.

"So you can talk to your invisible cat?"

"Just go, Tara. I've had enough of you."

"*Just go, Tara,*" she mocked in return.

"I don't have time for this today." I threw my arms up in exasperation, revealing the vial in my hand.

"What does the weirdo have today?" Tara said as she noticed the bottle.

"It's nothing. Leave me alone." I began to walk away, but Tara grabbed my arm. I whipped around, wild with rage.

"I said leave me alone, Tara. I think you'd be wise to listen to me today."

Tara flinched, put off by my newfound bravery. "Whatever, Gross Grace. No wonder you don't have any friends."

Thinking of the thousands of spirits waiting for me at the wall, I let out a loud laugh. "I have tons of friends, Tara."

"One. You have one friend, Gross Grace. And Bain isn't exactly a winner," Tara taunted. An evil little smile flashed on her face and then she flung herself at me, grabbing desperately for the vial of mermaid hair. Caught off-guard, I lost my grip. Tara snatched up the bottle.

She turned away from me and read the aged label aloud. "Mermaid hair. Really, mermaid hair? You're crazier than I thought, Gross Grace."

Anger flooded through my body. For years, Tara had tortured me. For years, I had tried to let it go. I was done letting it go.

"Maybe I am," I said softly, my eyes stormy slits of searing anger. "What are you going to do about it?" I stepped close to Tara, my nose inches from my tormentor's.

"Okay, Gross Grace, no need to get all weird on me," she said, her voice cracking.

"Too late," I said flatly. I raised my hand over my head and concentrated on Tara. Tara rose off the ground a few inches. She let out a high-pitched howl.

"It's time you left me alone, Tara. I am more than just weird. I am weird and powerful. And I've had enough," I said, still holding Tara in the air with my mind.

I let Tara drop to the ground and turned my focus to the vial of mermaid hair. With one flick of my eyes, it flew out of Tara's hands and into my own. I ran my fingers over the smooth glass and slipped it into the pocket of my gray hoodie. Tara stayed on the concrete, unable to comprehend our encounter. I stepped closer and towered over her.

"If you tell anyone about this, they won't believe you. No one will ever think that geeky Grace could have magical powers. It sounds insane when you say it, doesn't it?" I put my hands on my hips as I took another step closer to Tara. "You will keep this little incident to yourself; otherwise, *you* will be the loser at school, Tara. They'll think you're crazy. You will leave me alone from here on out, or I will make your life as miserable as you've made mine the past four years. Do you understand?"

Tara nodded timidly, the bottom lip of her open mouth quivering.

"Good. Now go home, Tara."

Tara got up gingerly, wearing an expression of utter shock.

I waved my hand in the direction of her house.

"Scoot."

Tara turned and sprinted down the street, glancing wide-eyed over her shoulder as she rounded the corner toward her house.

I turned to Midnight and laughed. "Looks like we showed her, Kitty-Cat. I'm so glad you were still here with me when Tara finally got what she deserved."

Midnight purred proudly.

GOODBYE GHOSTS

When we'd almost made it to the town wall, I stopped and looked at Midnight. My triumph over Tara had nearly made me forget how grief-stricken I was, but as we approached the spot on which the curse would be broken, pain flooded my heart.

"I guess this is it, Kitty-Cat. Thanks for everything," I said, suppressing my tears.

Midnight mewed and let out a long, blissful purr. I swallowed hard, held my head high, and rounded the corner. All of the ghosts waited for me. Spirits covered every inch of the wall. Ghosts filled the grassy field. The air above teemed with translucent gray apparitions. There was not a space unoccupied by a spirit.

"Hi, everyone," I said to the group of ghouls. "It seems Polly got my message out. Today's the day, friends. It's time you all went to the Light where you belong." My voice wobbled a bit as I tried not to cry.

Within seconds, the spirits surrounded me. Bartholomew Foster bellowed goodbye. Mrs. Mooney reminded me to always stand tall. A group of giggling little girl ghosts gave me cold hugs. One after another, the spirits of Tansy said their goodbyes. With each goodbye, my heart grew heavier and heavier.

Finally, only Thomas, Jenni, and Polly waited for their final moments with me. I might have been an only child, but these three ghosts were my siblings, at least in my heart. Tears streamed down my face as I choked back a sob. Thomas approached me first.

"You saved us. Thank you, my friend. It's been a pleasure to watch you grow up. Goodbye, little Grace." He smiled at me in the proud, big-brotherly way he often did.

"Goodbye, Thomas. Thanks for always looking out for me," I told him, my voice cracking. He nodded to Jenni, who floated forward.

"Gracie! I'm going to miss you so much! It's been totally rad to hang out with you for so long. Thank you for always being there when I missed my family. I was so lonely before you were born, but you made it better here." Jenni leaned in to give me a chilly hug goodbye, and Polly wafted over to me.

"Grace," Polly began to cry. "You've been my family since you were born. Not since I was alive have I felt so close to someone. I can never thank you enough for that or for what you're about to do. I love you."

"Love you like my dead sister, Pol," I whispered for the final time.

I looked for Midnight, but I couldn't seem to find him in the crowd. I began to panic. My palms sweaty and my heart pounding, I pushed through the crowd. I needed one last moment with my cat. After a few minutes of fruitless searching, I decided maybe it was for the best. I didn't think I could break the curse while looking into his yellow eyes. It would be too hard. Maybe he felt the same way.

I stepped up to the opening in the wall, just outside of Tansy's border, trying hard to stand as close as possible to the spot I remembered Lavina being.

Right as I opened my mouth to speak, a wispy white ghost I'd never seen before appeared in front of me. Her long, flowing hair looked vaguely familiar. A realization struck me.

"Lavina?" I whispered.

"Yes, Grace. Thank you for fixing my biggest mistake. My soul couldn't leave Tansy because I was too overridden with guilt. I was never cursed, but I was never at peace. When you break this curse, you'll free me, too. I've been hiding in the shadows for centuries."

She turned to the ghosts. "I never meant for this. I thought I'd failed to curse you. I know forgiveness is too much to ask for. I've made such a horrible mess of your afterlives."

The field filled with murmurs and exclamations.

"I read your journal. I know you were hurting. We all make mistakes when we're in pain," I told the old spirit.

She moved a bit closer. "I'd like to be by your side as you end what I started."

I nodded. "I'd be honored."

Gazing at the grateful ghosts, I began to speak. "Long ago, a curse was made, and now is the time for it to end." Tears fell hot on my cheeks, and my chin trembled as I spoke, but I continued, loud and clear. "This town's curse shall fade, and a new era shall begin. With the hair of a mermaid and the middle name of a fairy—Esmeralda—I free Tansy from the *Curse of Trapped Souls*."

The urge to see everything washed over me. Gazing at all the spirits who'd surrounded me every day of my life, I tried to take it all in, so I'd remember their faces forever. I took the vial out of my pocket and opened it to reveal the single strand of mermaid hair. Holding it up for the ghosts to see, I took a few steps forward and set it on the wall.

I moved back a few steps and waited. Within seconds, the spirits swirled all around me, forming a cloud of spiraling specters.

"I see it!" one voice called.

"The Light! It's so beautiful!" cried another.

"Is that you, Grammy?" a third voice squealed. I was positive that the third voice was Jenni Duncan.

One by one, the spirits disappeared. As each moved on to the next life, a light flashed in the sky. Some ghosts left green lights, other spirits left silver lights, and a few left pink lights, but they all made their beautiful marks on the dusky sky. I knew that the town would talk about this forever—the night the sky lit up.

Within a few minutes, I was alone. It was a kind of alone I'd never been in my life. Never before had I known that there would not be a ghost waiting for me upon my return home. I felt entirely empty. A void unlike any I'd ever known consumed me.

I hung my head and began to walk home, weeping with each painful breath.

MIDNIGHT RISES

About a block into my walk home, I found Bain beside me. He took my hand and held it in his own. "I went to your house, and your mom told me what you were doing," he told me. "I would have gone with you."

I sniffed. "I needed to do it myself. But I'm so glad you're here now."

"Are you okay?" he asked.

"No. But I will be," I said, trying to convince myself as much as Bain.

"Yeah, you will. You have the Mages of Nixie on your side now. And me."

It was difficult to be sure in the twilight, but I thought I saw Bain blush.

"Thank you," I said.

He wrapped his arm around my shoulder, pulling me in so close that my face brushed against his soft hoodie, and we walked toward Willow Way. I may have lost my ghosts, but at least I wouldn't be totally alone. I had Bain. On our way past the now-closed bakery, we stopped and sat at the wrought iron table out front. We stayed there and talked for an hour or so. As sad as I was, I welcomed the chance to talk to a living person.

The sky grew darker, and Bain said he needed to go home. He

hugged me, wrapping his arms tightly around me as if he could squeeze my sorrow away.

"The ghosts have departed this plane, but I'm here for you. I'll see you soon."

My gaze stayed on Bain as he walked away into the twilit town before I turned to walk the short distance to my house. The silence of a ghostless town was suffocating. Each step toward home felt heavier and heavier. I rounded the corner on to Willow Way and took in the sight of a home that had always been haunted. Inside, the purple Victorian was filled with loving, living people, but it looked empty in my eyes. I took a deep breath as I forced myself to climb the steps onto the porch. The top stair creaked as if in protest. My grip shaky on the brass knob, I opened the door to my new reality.

Inside, I found Mom pacing the living room, and my dad and grandparents sitting on the sofa. Dad held his head in his hands, his dark hair a wild mess as if he'd been running his hands through it for hours. Grandpa grabbed Grandma's hand, and his mouth gaped as he saw me enter the room. I realized how pale he looked, so unlike himself.

"Did it work?" Mom asked.

"It did," I replied softly.

"They're all gone?" Dad asked.

"Every single one of them."

"Are you okay?" Grandma asked, setting her hand on my shoulder.

"No," I told them honestly.

Grandpa stepped forward, placing his wrinkled hand on my shoulder. "Thank you, Grace. When it's my time—and the great news is that the doctors say I beat the cancer again, so that won't be for a long time—I won't be trapped here. I can go to the Light. Just not yet."

I pulled Grandpa into a tight hug, breathing in his familiar scent, tears forming in my eyes yet again. At least these were tears of relief instead of sadness. Releasing Grandpa, I felt dizzy with emotion. I needed to be alone.

"I think I'd like to go to my room now."

The adults exchanged a glance. Mom pulled me into a hug and whispered, "Take all the time you need."

I sprinted up the stairs and threw my door shut. I flung myself onto my bed and let out a sorrowful sob. Sometimes doing the right thing hurts horribly. The weight of saying goodbye to the ghosts hung over me.

I hid my face in my pillow and let my feelings flow out of me as each tormented tear fell. *Get it together, Grace,* I thought. *You can't cry forever.* A meow met my ear—Midnight's meow.

Great. Now I'm hallucinating. My pillow wiggled as something patted at it. Finally, I lifted my face to find Midnight staring at me. I sprung up from the bed.

"I thought you were gone, Kitty-Cat!" I squealed.

Much to my surprise, the cat spoke. "I couldn't leave you."

"Wait, you're talking. I *have* gone nuts. Oh, no. Oh, no, no..."

"No, you haven't, Grace. I'm a cat, but I was the pet of a powerful witch. Lavina. She bewitched me to make me speak long ago. I was so upset about what she did to the town of Tansy that I stayed after I passed away to try to help break the curse. I was never bound by that curse. It only affects humans."

"Why didn't you speak before now?"

"I have, actually. Who do you think kept going on about the mirror?"

I contemplated what the ghostly kitty was telling me. "But, I broke the curse. Why are you still here?"

"I'm here for *you*, Grace," he said as he rubbed against me and purred. "I've been in this town for more than three hundred years. What's one more lifetime with a friend like you?"

"Won't you fade away like the others?"

"Animal's souls are different. I could stay at least a hundred years longer. Most of us live shorter lives, but in some sort of cosmic balance, we get longer afterlives."

Tears of joy slid down my cheek. "Thank you, Midnight. I'm so glad you're still here."

"You asked me to stay until the end, friend, and your end won't come for a long, long time."

My heart pulsed with delight. I'd broken the curse. I'd made a few friends. Tara wasn't going to be bothering me anymore. Best of all, I still had Midnight.

Life was good.

29 OCTOBER

-Two Months Later-

The October breeze was crisp on my skin as I walked the short distance to Tansy School, leaves crunching underfoot. Midnight floated by my side as I headed down Willow Way, wearing a gray wool scarf and carrying my schoolbooks in a heavy silver backpack. The ghost cat rarely spoke these days. As it turned out, he much preferred to meow, but every once in a while, he and I chatted a bit. And, as he'd promised, he never left my side.

He'd been with me on my first day of seventh grade six weeks earlier. It had been the first school day in many years in which my stomach hadn't turned with fear at the thought of encountering Tara. It also had been the first day in which I had walked through the doors of Tansy School with living friends by my side. Bain and I had become inseparable. Over the summer, he'd taken me to a few of the gatherings of the Mages of Nixie, where I'd become friends with a mage in the eighth grade named Amelia, and gotten to know Sophia and her younger sister, Hannah, a bit better. On the first day of school, I entered the school building with my small band of mages. I barely noticed Tara skulking in the corners.

Midnight meowed as we turned onto Peach Street, alerting me to

Bain's presence. Bain usually walked to school with me. The kids at school had started calling Bain my boyfriend. Neither of us ever brought up the subject of dating, but my stomach filled with butterflies when I met him that morning.

"Hey, Grace!" Bain smiled when he saw me.

"Hi!" My face broke out into a matching grin.

"We need you. After school. There's an issue at the church that needs a spirittalker's expertise."

My heart skipped a few beats. Life in Tansy had changed so much since the ghosts went into the Light. I missed the spirits fiercely. I longed to tell Polly Hansen the latest town gossip or for Thomas Meyer to play pranks at school, but I knew that their spirits were finally resting in peace. I had to remind myself of this daily. As happy as I was to have my new living friends, I often missed spending my time with the dead.

It can't be one of my ghosts, can it? How? But if it isn't, then who is it? Oh, let it be Polly. My thoughts swirled with doubts and possibilities.

"Of course. We'll head over as soon as the last bell rings. What's going on?" My voice didn't mask my excitement.

Bain and I continued down the street together, heads close as we discussed in a whisper the trouble at the church. Midnight wafted around us and listened knowingly as we made afternoon ghost-hunting plans. It was as if he knew that we had our work cut out for us. I knew that whatever happened, he would be there, ready to help, however he could.

He'd made a promise, after all.

ACKNOWLEDGMENTS

I have been so blessed in the process of writing this book. As always, my husband and kids have been so supportive of my writing process. Thanks so much for all that you do.

I had some amazing support from my first readers. Liz, April, and Debbie, thank you so much for all of your feedback. You helped shape and polish this book more than you know.

I was so blessed to have Lindsay Flanagan for an editor. Thank you so much for finding Grace in the #PitMad slush and bringing her to life in this story.

My agent, Jessica Reino, joined me late in the process of this book, but has been so helpful. Thank you, Jessica. I look forward to working with you on many future projects.

To the whole team at Immortal Works- thank you for giving this book a chance. I'm so excited to be an Immortal Works author.

ABOUT THE AUTHOR

Stephenie is the author of *Grace's Ghosts* and the *Nellie Nova* series. Semi-nomadic, she currently lives near Raleigh, North Carolina. Stephenie's roots are in the Puget Sound region in Washington State, and she spent many years living outside of Dallas, Texas. She spends her days writing, teaching creative writing, and homeschooling her three kids. Fueled by lots and lots of coffee, Stephenie spends her free time hanging out with her family, playing with her rescue dogs, Ravenpaw and Leviosa, hiking, and traveling. You can find out more about Stephenie and her work at www.stepheniepeterson.com.

This has been an
Immortal Production

CPSIA information can be obtained
at www.ICGtesting.com
Printed in the USA
BVHW030236110920
588600BV00001B/252